Tabloid Nation

John Schasny

PublishAmerica
Baltimore

First printing

ISBN: 1-4137-6990-X (softcover)
ISBN: 978-1-4489-1268-1 (hardcover)
PUBLISHED BY PUBLISHAMERICA, LLLP
www.publishamerica.com
Baltimore

Printed in the United States of America

For all of you

I t is as if everything was waited until right now. Only in here we are made up of untitled songs, snatches of this and that, the congregation of our collected selves. Unwhole, then whole again.

Astral displacement.

You can only count on this, brother: Rise, fall, be quick.

Move and touch. Touch and move.

Step aside. Make a place for another.

An uneasy edge, like water moving, slick as silt. Like cat scratches, and quick as Time. It's here and it's gone. Beaten feet in an ugly rain.

One. Two. Three.

The only message heard clear: We come from where we started, we go to where are.

*****

All this running and what has it got me? Zero to eternity, and one more crash site.

Rubberneckers no longer just slow down; they give political correctness the finger and park in the middle of the spattered gore. With a propulsive hunger, they scramble out of their vehicles, cameras in hand, duty bound to videotape the carnage, preserving the horror to share with friends over a beer, and maybe some kind bud. "This is a good one. You gotta see this one."

Voyeuristic gluttony.

Looking, hunting, her Kodak throwaway camera at the ready, Holsie Colldren clomps over twisted and mangled auto parts, splashes through an oily soup of antifreeze, gasoline and blood.

The gruesome remains of a young girl, hit while crossing the street, bone-broken and damaged beyond any kind of repair, becomes the subject of amateur photographers, many of whom will attempt to sell their photographs to supermarket tabloids and local newspapers.

"All these books." Holsie marvels at the books scattered everywhere, the streaked pages of words strewn amongst the wreckage. She snaps a picture. The flash does not go off. She frowns at the camera, gives it a slap.

Slack-jawed lookie-loos prevent paramedics and EMS personnel from getting to the site. A horn honks, a siren wails. Nobody moves.

The burly truck driver who mowed her down and who will later he identified as Brahulyo Saucedo stands alone, himself cut in many places, weeping uncontrollably, a cigarette between his fingers, burning his flesh.

A man sidles up next to Holsie. "Is that the guy who did it?"

"Where?" She swings her cardboard camera around, ready to shoot anything that moves.

"Did you do it? You the one that hit her?"

Brahulyo does not answer. Maybe he does not hear the man's question.

"I'm getting it on tape just in case." The man shoulders his video camera. "Powerful stuff," he mutters, advancing on the shaken and distraught Brahulyo, whose private hell is no longer private. "This shit is off the hook."

"Oh my god!" someone screams. "A dog!"

The trophy hunters gasp, rush to the voice, swarm over the soggy, sticky corpse of what might have been a terrier. Some of the tourists sob. Some kneel, reach out, but no one touches the dead, broken animal.

"Was it the girl's?" Holsie wants to know.

Many are upset that it's just a puppy.

Brahulyo turns his back, leans unsteadily against his 16-wheeler, tortured with grief. The ash from his cigarette flies into his hair. He does not feel it burning his scalp.

Flares are ignited, lighting the scene with an eerie and surreal smoky glow. A scavenger hunt in candy land. They wander through the smoke in a ragged file. When they bump into one another they excuse themselves, then move along carefully over the mine field of souvenirs. Flashbulbs explode. Little dotty puffs of bright white go off in the dark, memorizing the carnage and transferring it to film for later viewing.

"This camera sucks," Holsie grumbles, "the flash isn't working."

A young man takes a look at her camera, explains that there is no flash attachment. The throwaway model she bought is for bright outdoor use only. A day camera.

"Well, crap," Holsie tells him. "That doesn't do nothin' for me. Now what."

The young man shrugs, spots something. He bends over to pick it up. "Check this out," he says, then walks off without showing his souvenir to anybody.

A state trooper comes by and motions for Holsie to leave the area.

"Why, I'm not doing anything," she complains.

Someone coughs.

"You better take care of that thing," a voice warns.

Dewey and the boys drive by slowly, tires crunching over broken glass and shards of metal. Dewey is convinced that if more people would learn how to functify, the world would be a better place. But Dewey has no idea how to reach total functification and must rely on others to lead him to nirvana.

"Comin' through," he says. Dewey is not just making small talk; he drives through the middle of everything.

It begins to rain. A paramedic hauls a tarp out to cover up the dead girl.

The state trooper, dulled by years of destruction and death, waves the old Pontiac through. Dewey and the boys lean out, survey the littered roadway. Dewey scrambles for one last look. "Dude. She's hot. For reals."

The boys scramble all over one another to get a glimpse of the one-time show before the curtain comes down.

Cameras flash, video cameras roll. The memory of the tragedy is recorded, saved. The horror is documented and preserved, collected by complete strangers who will never learn the identities of their targets or appreciate the chain of sorrow and grief their passing will initiate.

"What do you suppose is gonna happen to all those books," Holsie wants to know.

As if everything was waited until right now.

Hunters and gatherers all.

*****

Nobody can find the crop circles. Rumor, hearsay, poorly drawn maps add to the confusion. Kwame seems to be in charge at the moment, although nobody knows how that came to be.

"Well? Where are they?" Holsie wants to see the crop circles that have been promised.

"They for damn sure ain't here." Kwame stares into the nothingness that is not crop circles.

"Those guys over there said this was the place," someone suggests.

Hopeful eyes wander to Dewey and the boys, drinking cans of beer in their Pontiac, the convertible top down.

Kwame's not buying it. "Them dumbasses? Don't believe nothin' Dewey says about nothin'!"

Patient and hopeful, the faithful stare with Kwame into the void of empty expanse.

Finally someone suggests the obvious. "We could try somewheres else."

"No shit, Sherlock," comes a voice.

Giggles.

Someone farts loudly. One of Dewey's boys?

More laughter.

Kwame calculates they need to cover another hundred miles to the campground. But he's been wrong before.

A discussion on who's going where. Holsie is nuking a plate of nachos in her R.V. and she offers to share.

Another fart.

"Is that a no?" Dewey and the boys cackle loudly.

"We can do without that." Kwame glares in the general direction of the fart-makers.

The erotically strange Candelaria "Candy" Chacon presents her skinny self to the gathering. An alleged former cocaine mule for the Mexican cartel, Candy is an excitement-weirdness junky. A tiny T-shirt barely covers her little-girl breasts. Her navel is pierced, a colorful tattoo peeps out from the front of her short-shorts. She drags a backpack filled with everything she owns.

"Can someone give me a ride?" she asks.

Dewey wants to know where she's going.

"Same as everybody else," she tells him. "The crop stompers."

"Get in," Dewey says, starting the Pontiac and revving the engine. "This waiting around is not saltin' my cracker."

"Yeah. This sucks major penis," concurs one of the boys.

"Wouldn't do that if I was you." Kwame's admonition falls on deaf ears. Candy is already in the back seat of the big red muscle car.

Dewey and the boys are the first to break ranks and drive off. As they roar past, a voice from the car: "More cheese, please."

Somebody mutters something about a "screw job" and the crowd slowly disperses. They will drive until they find a campground. Holsie will eat most of the nachos herself, while her husband, confined to a wheelchair, downloads porn off the net, an instrument he derisively refers to as "the corporate whore machine."

It's an ensemble road movie. A crap factory.

Get your freak on.

For reals.

Ask Stump and Martha Sittingdown. An empty large-mouth orange juice jug has become their surrogate child. They put a bib on it, feed it, lug it around in a homemade papoose. Rub it liberally with SPF 30 sunscreen. Celebrate it's "best if used by" date every year.

Somewhere in New Mexico, while scooping up buckets of sacred guano from the holy bat caves, baby Sittingdown suddenly developed a case of the furies. Stump grabbed it from Martha, turned it upside down, shook it violently. Milk, food, water, the crap they'd been feeding it and the enzymes that had broken it all down, splattered out onto the floor of the cave, tainting the consecrated bat droppings.

"What did baby do!" Stump demanded an answer. "What!"

Baby Sittingdown crapped itself.

"Look at our boy! All over!"

With the lid unscrewed, the sickening mush of reeking viscid alkaline fluid was released in a deadly spray of oozy discharge, covering everyone.

Someone says, "Maybe he vomited."

"Dude, watch yer kid."

"Did him bommit?"

Stump, in a rage of his own, hurled his plastic-jug baby against a wall covered with the sacrosanct shit.

"Then you can sit in it until we're done!"

Martha Sittingdown wails inconsolably. Baby is silent. Accusatory glares from nearly everyone else. The parade restarts.

"Oh, for Christ sake, he couldn't even feel it!" Stump gathers up the precious poop, ignoring both mother and child.

Hundreds of pounds of shit are eventually excavated and baby is forgiven. Everything comes up smelling like roses.

The caravan rolls on.

*****

Walbert and Briola have no children.

They fell in with the caravan when it rolled through Spanish Pork, Utah. Briola's mother, Zinaida, complains in the back seat, for the umpteenth time, that because she had no time to pack, she has nothing to wear. She has no money. She wants to go home.

Walbert, for the umpteenth time, offers to let her out at the side of the road. This quiets Zinaida for another hundred miles.

Briola wants to drink from the spring that is said to refresh and stimulate the ovaries. She wants her tubes reanimated. She wants to regenerate her womb, and she wants to have children. Not like Stump and Martha Sittingdown, but a real-life baby.

The fecund spring waters await and Briola wants to become fertile, wants to taste the sweetness of the efficacious fluid that will cause life to erupt in her loins.

Briola is 46 years old. She has no idea that Walbert's sperm cannot swim or see. That no matter how much spring water she drinks, she will never bear children.

Not Walbert's anyway.

The car is hot and there is no air-conditioning. Briola worries the heat is making her uterus shrink and wither even more. She doesn't give a thought to Walbert's out-of-work testicles. She makes him stop at every convenience store along the way so she can purchase a chilled bottle of drinking water, which she will place between her legs. She wants Niagara, after being told of its tantalizing properties, but has been unable to find the blue-bottled elixir anywhere.

Zinaida sulks. Her hair is whipped to shreds by the wind from the open window. She has no comb to repair the damage.

The front speakers do not work. Walbert turns the volume up so he can hear the music coming from the back, where Zinaida sits, muttering to herself. She is unhappy and wants to go back home.

"Can't hear you back there," Walbert says.

Zinaida asks him to repeat himself.

"Only the rear speakers work! Gotta blast it or I can't hear anything!"

Zinaida holds her hair down with both hands to ease the whipping lariats that have been assaulting her for miles. Days. "What?"

"I can't hear shit up here!" Walbert smiles wickedly. He steps on the gas.

"We're almost there," Briola offers.

"That's what you said about the Doomsday Asteroid. Where's that? Same as the Fountain of Youth. It does not exist."

"You can't see something that hasn't arrived yet."

Zinaida is frustrated. "It's not five yet?"

"We will see the asteroid when it gets here. Then it's on to New Land."

Walbert considers putting Zinaida on a bus in the next town. They agree they will decide what to do with her when they stop for gas.

They talk like Zinaida isn't there.

"None of this crap is real you know." Zinaida's words fall on deaf ears.

Walbert cranks up the radio. "Free Bird."

"Did you just call me a turd?"

Walbert looks at Briola and shakes his head. "Like talkin' to a milking stool."

"You're the fool," Zinaida says, and pretends to fall asleep.

*****

The conspiracy buffs, the videotape armies, step-families and trailer trash. They're all here. A perverse paparazzi living off phone cards, maxed-out plastic, and fast food. Betting on who will be the next to go postal.

Peeping Toms and Tammys. Rubberneckers waiting for the next freak show, their tedium and boredom chips cashed in for a few days, weeks, months on the road. Their chance to see and be seen; hear and be heard. To belong. Trying to get jiggy widdit.

Gettin' their freak on.

Opening their pores to the possibility of pure strange. Their only reality.

These people are my television.

*****

Bob Bluitt is fresh out of rehab. Before that he was living with a prostitute and her three kids. He was intrigued with the idea of getting for free what others had to pay for. What he didn't count on was the endless parade of johns showing up at the apartment around the clock with cash to pay for what he was getting for free.

The truth of the matter is he wasn't getting any at all.

Frustrated and jealous, his dipsomania eventually got the best of him and he woke up one morning, naked and bruised, sleeping it off in the back of his Honda.

Bob now lives in the Hatchback Hotel. He has no driver's license. He wants to get to Mount Nirvana before the big monkey takeover. He is fearful of black helicopters and wants to create an army of submissive Barbie look-alikes.

Bob believes he will be cured. Bob also believes he will become famous.

*****

The crop circles are only a stop on the way, not the final destination. Rumor is that the geometric patterns will point the way to the Doomsday Asteroid, which ultimately will lead to New Land, and so for this reason it becomes more than just a diversion. It is a must-see.

The route has become schizophrenic and circuitous—an allegorical microcosm of the group itself—with unanticipated twists and turns precipitated by spontaneous insight and extemporaneous hunches. Kwame's map is a pastiche of hatch marks, red and blue lines crisscrossing drunkenly over roadways and interstates. The dizzying coordinates make little sense to the untrained eye, but Kwame has been unyielding in his resolve. In spite of all the confusion, this colorful patchwork will guide him—them—to their imminent goal.

Serendipity has been a useful tool in their arsenal, and when two hitchhikers exchange information for some of Holsie Colldren's microwave burritos, Kwame knows they are close.

A snap decision is made.

The seekers, their vehicles strung out over a mile, decide to reverse direction and set their compasses for Kansas.

Two more days on the road, another unexpected directional tip, and they find themselves instead in Nebraska, surrounded by cornfields, but strung out, single file, on a frontage road, at a virtual standstill.

Stump radios Kwame on his CB, wanting to know what's going on, but since they are the only two with radios, Kwame has turned his down, electing instead to use the more conventional means of communication—the cell phone.

"What's going on?" Holsie wants to know. She's in the rear of the pack, blind to what's going on a mile ahead of them.

"Get parked and get up here," Kwame instructs her. He flash-dials the others, but all lines are busy. When he hangs up, his phone immediately rings.

"Talk to me," Kwame barks into his Nokia.

"Is Peppy there?" The voice is disguised. Kwame hears laughter in the background.

"Who?"

"Peppy," the voice says.

"Peppy who?"

"Roni."

Kwame doesn't get it. "Peppy Roni? You're looking for Peppy Roni?"

"Yes. Peppy."

Kwame suspects it is Dewey and his crew, and he regrets not spending the extra money to get caller i.d.

"You're tying up the line with this crap?"

"No. Peppy—"

Kwame hangs up, decides to pay the one-time fee by using his *69 feature. He calls the number back.

"Chota's Bar and Grill," a voice answers. More snickering in the background.

"Dewey—"

The caravan begins to roll. Traffic is moving and Kwame disconnects himself from the pranksters on the other end of the line, only to be disappointed by the vagary of stop-and-go traffic.

Kwame ignores the ringing of his telephone. In his rearview mirror he can see Holsie Colldren, red-faced, panting, lurching towards the front of the line on foot, her legs burned crimson from the scorching sun.

A motorcyclist makes his way against the traffic. Kwame flags him down.

"What's going on up there?"

"It's awesome, man!" The motorcyclist keeps going, barely misses Holsie Colldren, who has fallen down and sits on the rough asphalt, trying to catch her breath.

Kwame strains to see what lies ahead of them. He is determined to stay in his vehicle and not lose his place in line. He inches forward. His pulse races.

Kwame's cell phone rings. Against his better judgment, he answers. "It's your nickel."

"Where the hell is Holsie! What happened to her!"

Kwame can't remember the name of Holsie's disabled husband. He checks his rearview mirror. Holsie is on all fours, trying to get to her feet.

"I'm sitting back here while every Tom, Dick and Harry, is cutting in front of me! You people know I can't drive this piece of shit! Where the hell is she!"

"I can see her from here," Kwame tells him.

"See her *where?*"

The pickup truck in front of Kwame pulls forward unexpectedly, and Kwame gooses it to keep up with him.

The husband with no name is frustrated and concerned. "*Where!*"

A young girl suddenly appears at Kwame's window. She is wearing a blaze-orange hunter's vest and is clutching a fistful of cash. She looks in the car, smiling like a carved pumpkin. Her breath smells like Twizzlers.

"How many?"

"How many what?" Kwame wants to know.

"Is Holsie with you or not!" Holsie's husband sounds frantic. Kwame has forgotten about the nameless voice on the other end of his Nokia.

"How many tickets for the maze."

"What maze?"

"The corn maze." The young girl smiles beatifically, points at something.

Kwame leans, looks up through his windshield. He wonders how he could have missed the sign before.

WORLD'S LARGEST CORN MAZE!

The words tear at Kwame, taunting his leadership abilities. Kwame can think of nothing to say. His stock has plummeted.

"One."

"Seven-fifty," the smiling face says, her words wrapped around the sweet cherry scent of the Twizzlers.

"Christ and beans! Will you tell me what is going on!" Holsie's no-name spouse will have to find out for himself.

*****

The corn maze/crop circle fiasco results in a fractious split at the Colorado border. The not-so-faithful elect to make their way to New Mexico to corroborate a flurry of Virgin Mary sightings, and Kwame, more determined than ever to right his wrongs, convinces the others that they will be viewing the Doomsday Asteroid in a matter of days.

Kwame prays all night long, trying to cut a deal with his Creator. He knows it's only a matter of time, but he needs the insurance. Every decision he makes is now evaluated and weighed by the others, who are fast becoming critical purveyors of his leadership abilities. As lion of this tabloid tribe, he cannot afford to be second-guessed. Not now.

Tick tock, tick tock.

Kwame is prepared to wait as long as he has to for the divine intervention that will save his ass, and he is flabbergasted when it comes to him eleven hours later in a truck stop diner on the outskirts of Loveland, Colorado.

Oris Kumke's identity was stolen when he made a credit card purchase off the Internet. His bank accounts were emptied and he lost his business. His wife left him and managed to take all three of their vehicles with her. When he tried to drown his sorrows in a local tavern, he was unable to pay his tab and his lights were immediately punched out. His short-term memory is faulty and many believe he suffers from Alzheimer's Disease.

Oris Kumke claims to hold the patent to a device that can recognize carbon-based life forms, but with his lousy credit rating and identity in contest, he cannot access his patent and his invention remains off the market.

Kwame was raised to believe that he who is given the most bears the greatest responsibility, so when he sees Oris Kumke sitting on a speed bump outside the diner, he offers to buy him a hot meal, and over chicken-fried steak and apple pie, Oris Kumke weaves his tale.

He can't remember if he was in Colorado or Wyoming at the time, but at a convention for UFO abductees, Oris Kumke watched as a young girl became host for an otherworldly presence who channeled through her to alert everyone in the auditorium about an event that would soon take place in the Rocky Mountains. The young girl, whose name he can no longer recall, went into a trance state and wrote specific details on a wet-erasure board. Oris Kumke was unable to read exactly what she wrote, owing to the fact that the IRS had seized his home and all the contents therein, which included his eyeglasses. He remembers it was by a lake and in the mountains, and that after the exact location was given, the child laid her hands upon several people in the room and healed them of varying ailments and disorders.

Oris Kumke followed this with a brief rant about how the government was trying to run people like him out of business. "That's their deal. Run the independents out. Gives me a pure case of the monkey nerves just thinking about it."

Kwame orders more coffee. He questions Oris Kumke delicately, not wanting to touch a nerve.

"So what are you doing here?

"Thanks to your generosity, I'm eating."

"No," Kwame elucidates, "what brings you here, to this diner. Today."

"Oh. Great place to get lost."

"At a roadside diner?"

"Well," Oris Kumke says between bites of apple pie, "I was gonna hitch a ride. Try and find that little girl, see if she could fix my eyes. I got no glasses."

Holsie Colldren is the last to arrive. She pushes her husband in his chair. He is angry with her and waves her away.

"Mad as a hornet," Holsie says, when she passes the booth. Her husband wheels himself to an empty table. Holsie follows, shaking her head and rolling her eyes.

"How will you do that?" Kwame wants to know.

"Just ask strangers for a ride, I guess." Oris Kumke pushes his empty plate away, asks Kwame if he can bum a smoke.

"Don't smoke," Kwame says. "No, I mean, how will you find the girl?"

Oris Kumke looks around the diner, squinting. "Well—" He points. "Could ask her, I guess."

The girl Oris Kumke has directed our attention to is seated alone in a booth. Barely five feet tall, with thick, abundant hair the color of chocolate. We stare at her fleshy lips, broad gumdrop of a nose. Her eyes only slightly darker than her hair. She has a tiny mole on her neck. The lobes of her ears are buttercups. The relaxed sweater conceals her breasts, but reveals delicate, freckled shoulders. She drinks a bottle of beer and writes furiously in a spiral notebook.

"And who is that?" Kwame wants to know.

"Duft."

Duft. The intonation of the word, even coming from Oris Kumke, undulates sweetly through the flat air of the diner.

Duft.

A turbulence of sugar inside the mouth. Say it with me.

Duft.

Cryptic. Mystical. Enigmatic. A euphonious blaze of hungering whispers.

Hear.

Duft.

Oris Kumke recognizes Duft from the convention hall where the young girl began channeling and trance-writing. At least he thinks it's her.

Kwame calls for a check, then he and Oris Kumke approach Duft. Words are exchanged and she offers them the other side of the booth.

Three hours later we're on the road. Kwame and Oris Kumke, me and Duft. She needed a ride.

*****

Duft speaks and a strange language floats around us. Everything else matters little.

In another place, when she was an unbled pre-teen, four roughnecks took her apart, and under their fists she gave each of them pieces of her self. Uninterrupted and regular as clockwork, the once-sweet air turned thick as mud as they climbed along the comet's length of her, leaving her in rags and raving, the ghost of another. Changed.

She stutters on.

I pick apart the odd dialect, learn how she was hollowed out in mute disarray, her strength tested time and time again. Every detail whisper-spoken in a sibilant rush of candied breath.

She says kicking strangers is not as hard as it looks.

I only have to nod.

On top of the Continental Divide we eat the two hard-boiled eggs that Duft bought at the diner.

All night long we drive, and share our personal histories.

*****

Duft corroborates much of what Oris Kumke has told Kwame. We need to get to an isolated lake in California before the 15th. Her notebook contains the words the young girl wrote while in her trance: *2 days hence, Hidden Lake, Fireball from the Sky.*

There is a second message which she is reluctant to share.

But I have learned something about Duft. I know her Big Secret, and I will not share it with anyone.

Olfactory acuity.

You see, Duft is hard-wired to be scent-responsive. The organs of smell in most people are made up of tissue about the size of a postage stamp, but through some quirky cell-splitting mishap that occurred while Duft was still just a nameless zygote curled up in her comfortable little sac of amniotic fluid, her olfactory membranes mutated into roughly the size of a silver dollar, and this is worth more than money to me.

Duft carries fresh sweet basil leaves somewhere on her person at all times.

The roses of our time spent together grow deep.

*****

Kwame telephones everyone left in the group. The nervous excitement in his voice is palpable. This close to the realization of everyone's super-dream and it is now or never. We push off for the final leg of our journey, heeding Kwame's admonition that there will be no patience for those who cannot keep up.

Kwame strikes out in earnest. It has been decided that the

channeling child did not mean the lake everyone is looking for was hidden; rather, a careful study of a topographical map bought at the diner reveals an actual Hidden Lake.

Kwame is ecstatic, to say the least. He acknowledges to his Creator that, yes, we are fat and lazy as a nation and, no, we do not do our homework as citizens or Christians, but this miraculous answer to his prayers has put him back in the driver's seat. He promises to be a better citizen and to be more charitable to the others. He includes Dewey and his boys in this pledge of benevolence.

Kwame vows to attend church the following Sunday and swears aloud that he will take 10 percent of whatever he has in his pocket at the time. Relieved of what he considers his evangelical payback, Kwame settles in behind the wheel, fueled by a sense of self-righteousness and a full tank of gas.

"We are going to the promised land," he declares. "And you can take that to the bank."

Kwame is gettin' jiggy widdit.

Oris Kumke has fashioned a sign which proclaims, DIVISTATION OR JUBILEE? WASH AWAY CONFUSION! THIS WAY!

The arrow is pointing in the wrong direction, lending the impression that they are *running away* from the declaration of promised salvation.

Walbert and Briola find a temporary solution to their problem. They pawn Zinaida off on Holsie and her husband, which is fine with Zinaida. Holsie's R.V. has a fully equipped kitchen and a color TV, and she is finally able to watch her soaps again.

Holsie drives the lumbering home on wheels while Zinaida tends to Holsie's man. It is her job to keep everyone supplied with hot snacks whipped up in the microwave and to make sure that Holsie's husband's wheels are chocked so he doesn't roll out of control while making their way along the steep and winding mountain roads.

When Walbert and Briola pass them on a narrow hairpin curve, Zinaida holds a plate of steaming chimichangas up to the window so they can covet the upgrade in her standard of living. Zinaida takes a deep breath, inhaling the aromatic essence of the nuked finger food. When Walbert's mouth begins to move, she draws the curtain closed.

"Lookin' out for number one—as always." Walbert seethes, and cranks up "Positively 4th Street" on the radio.

Holsie's husband works on his website, referring continually to his battered copy of *Websites for Dumbasses*. He tries to explain to Zinaida the complexities of his URL, but she becomes distracted by the game show host they are watching.

"He's stupid."

"Now how would you know that?"

"Look at him," Zinaida says. "He just looks stupid."

"He can't help that."

"Well, he shouldn't look that way. He shouldn't be on TV looking that way."

Holsie's husband can think of nothing else to say. "That's not nice."

"I don't care," Zinaida says. She makes her way to the cab and offers Holsie some chimichangas.

Holsie is stressed and sweats profusely. She is not used to mountain driving and complains that moments earlier someone almost cut her off. She is a nervous wreck and says that if they don't get out of the mountains soon, she is going to turn around and go to New Mexico. The Virgin Mary may still be there.

Holsie passes on the chimichangas, fearful of removing her hands from the steering wheel. She tells Zinaida they may have to drop out. The big R.V. is no match for the thin mountain air and she is the only one with a driver's license, so no one is able to provide relief from the stress of driving.

Zinaida does not want to leave the comfort of the well-equipped R.V. She washes her hair daily with herbal shampoo and Holsie has given her a new comb and brush set. They do two loads of laundry a day and there is more than enough food and carbonated soft drinks.

Zinaida plops in front of the small television.

"Looks like he's getting fat again, doesn't it? Look at his face. Ach, that asshole, I can't stand him. Sheesh. Give him the hook."

Holsie's husband suggests popping in a video.

Zinaida grabs a cassette at random and reads the handmade label. "I hate this guy. He makes me sick. I can't *stand* that man! When are they gonna get rid of him? You ever listen to the way he says his S's? Ach, I can't *stomach* that man!"

Holsie's husband turns on the radio.

"Is that Bing Crosby? Oh, I can't *stand* him! Especially knowing what I know about him…what he was. I can't stand that man! Him and Grace Kelly both. She couldn't act worth beans. But I liked her as a princess."

Holsie's husband turns off the radio.

Zinaida polishes off the chimichangas, then announces they will be having 15-bean soup for dinner.

Darkness comes early in the Rockies, but black of night will not stay this group from their appointed destiny. Kwame has seen to that.

While he maneuvers his vehicle through the twists and turns of the mountain passes, Oris Kumke operates a hood-mounted spotlight, picking out dangerous S-curves that lie in wait for them. Occasionally he blinds unsuspecting drivers in oncoming vehicles, but that's their problem. Oris Kumke has a job to do, and he knows Kwame is relying on his ability to pinpoint potential trouble spots.

They are a team.

The first directional sign for Hidden Lake brings a jubilant cry from Kwame and he immediately gets on the horn to the others. He calls Holsie first. Zinaida answers.

"Hello, who is this?" She suspects it might be Walbert, who called earlier, offering up a litany of profanities.

The steep canyon walls break up the cellular transmission, interrupting much of the conversation. Kwame does not know this.

"You guys ready for a miracle?" Kwame is giddy with anticipation.

"You can go to hell," Zinaida says, and terminates the call.

Nonplussed, Kwame calls the Sittingdowns. Someone answers, but he cannot understand a word they are saying.

"We're almost there," he tells the receiver of his staticky missive. "Get ready for a miracle."

More static. A scream. Then more static. Kwame suspects Baby Sittingdown is behaving badly.

Indifferent, he speed-dials Dewey.

"Martha's Whorehouse," a voice proclaims. "We feed 'em, you eat 'em."

Kwame has no time for this and hangs up. He calls Bob Bluitt, but his answering machine kicks in. Kwame hangs up.

Kwame's telephone rings.

"Get that," he tells Oris Kumke.

Oris Kumke picks up, fumbles with the small Nokia.

"Hello. Hello?" Oris Kumke listens for a long time. "Nobody there."

"You sure?"

"I don't hear nothin'. No, wait." Oris Kumke listens intently.

"Who is it?" Kwame wants to know.

Oris Kumke shrugs, holds out the telephone. "Bobby Bigdick."

"Who?"

Oris Kumke gets back on the horn. "Who?" he asks. "Now he says it's Nathan Nutsack."

"Don't tie up the line with that crap."

"What should I do?"

Kwame sighs as loud as he can, then says, "Hang up."

"How?" Oris Kumke stares at the small telephonic contraption.

"Just hit the button."

Oris Kumke wants to know which one. He presses a series of buttons, then drops the phone on the seat. The international operator patiently awaits the caller's request.

Kwame attempts to explain the allowable minutes available under his intricate calling plan but a herd of grazing deer in a small valley catches Oris Kumke's attention. He blinds them with the stultifying hood-lamp. Transfixed, the thin and sickly deer freeze and stare into the light.

Oris Kumke fumbles with something in his pants pocket. He rolls down his window.

"What's going on over there?" Kwame is nervous, and the cool mountain air is making him shiver.

"Just gettin' Bambi in the cross hairs is all. You kinda don't want to pull the trigger, but then again—price paid, lesson learned."

KA-BOOM!

A deafening blast from Oris Kumke's no-longer-concealed handgun bounces off canyon walls and mountains, reverberating in a series of mind-numbing echoes.

"Jesus Christ, what in God's holy name are you doing!" Kwame narrowly avoids slamming into a sheer rock cliff, over-corrects, then almost drives off the road. Behind them, the sounds of locked-up brakes, squealing tires and car horns.

"Pull over somewhere. I can have that thing dressed out in two hours."

"What the hell are you doing! You killed that deer?"

"You drove by so fast I couldn't tell. Pull over."

"No! We do not have time for this crap!" Kwame is nearly apoplectic. Oris Kumke is ruining everything.

"You're passing up an opportunity to feed this entire tribe is what you're doing."

"Forget the tribe," Kwame says.

"Oh, so it's all about you now."

Kwame drives past a sign which he was unable to read.

"What was that! What'd that sign say?"

"You got me," Oris Kumke says. He spins the spotlight behind them, tries to pick the deer out of the darkness. "You didn't see them, but they didn't look right."

"I have no earthly idea what you are talking about."

"Bambi! The deer!"

A horn honks, tires squeal. Somebody's blinded. A vehicle teeters dangerously from side to side, high beams flickering on and off in some kind of warning or cry for help.

Kwame's telephone rings.

"Want me to get that?"

"Leave it alone!" Kwame picks up the phone himself. "Tell me about it," he says into the receiver.

It's Bob Bluitt. "We're being shot at back here!"

Kwame thinks he says, "It's hot in here."

Kwame is rattled. "We're pulling over."

"The sooner the better," Oris Kumke says. "We gotta pack that thing outta here. It didn't look too healthy."

Kwame pulls onto a darkened side road. Once again, divine intervention has reached down and tapped him on the shoulder.

Framed in his high beams, a hand-painted sign.

WELCOME TO HIDDEN LAKE.

"It's not here," he hears Bob Bluitt say.

"Yes it is," he shouts into the phone, and hangs up.

Unable to contain his excitement, Kwame climbs out of his vehicle. He waves his arms, pinwheel fashion, at the others, encouraging them to follow him onto the darkened roadway.

"Our prayers have been answered," he tells whoever can hear him.

Dewey and his boys barrel past them, honking, chucking empty beer cans in their direction. Dewey yells something out, but Kwame does not hear. He will not allow Dewey to spoil the moment.

But something is not right. The Sittingdowns also keep going, waving and pointing. Then Holsie's R.V. Bob Bluitt rockets past them in the Hatchback Hotel, honking, flashing his lights.

Kwame goes back to his vehicle, trains the spotlight on the sign.

WELCOME TO HIDDEN LAKE. *Next Left 1/4 Mile.*

Dewey has beaten him at his own game. Again.

By the time Kwame and Oris Kumke catch up with the others, it's obvious they missed the boat. It is all over.

Police, forest rangers, and national guardsmen, keep everyone at bay. Whatever the event, it has already taken place. The area is now cordoned off with yellow crime scene tape. Go on home, folks, there's nothing to see.

Stick a fork in them. They're done.

Kwame insists on an explanation, but none is forthcoming.

Kwame and the others are disappointed beyond belief.

Oris Kumke is not surprised at all. It's the same old song—the government putting the screws to the little guy. Again.

Dewey and the boys have a mighty buzz on and when Dewey sees Kwame in tears, he can hardly keep a straight face.

"Assume the position: Face down, butt up!" Dewey taunts the tearful Kwame, tells him to take one for the team. Give it up for Uncle Sam and allow the government to "plant the flagpole."

"It's a big lie. Don't you get it?" Oris Kumke is bitter and does not care who knows it.

"Get what, Opie?"

Oris Kumke wants to know who said that. Nobody fesses up and that infuriates Oris Kumke. He yanks the antenna off Bob Bluitt's hatchback, snips the tip of it off with a pair of wire cutters, and fashions it into what he calls his Brooklyn Bullwhip. This group will never see the scorched earth, the huge hole in the ground, or know what caused it. Everyone is given three minutes to leave the area or face arrest. They are directed to a campground a mile away.

"Think you can find it without getting lost?" Dewey wants to know.

Kwame has had enough.

"Instead of bumpin' your gums and jackin' your jaws off, why don't you try directing your energy in a more positive vein for a once! You ain't helpin' matters with your smart-mouth attitude!"

"Why don't you smart-mouth this?" Dewey rubs his crotch. Even Candy laughs.

"Nice burn," she says.

Kwame gets back into his car. Oris Kumke slithers in beside him, his Brooklyn Bullwhip clenched tightly in his fist. As they back out onto the highway, Kwame catches a glimpse of Zinaida passing out bread sticks to the National Guardsmen.

"She's fuckin' feedin' 'em!" Kwame says in disbelief. "What ever."

Kwame wipes his eyes with his shirt sleeve and takes off in search of the campground.

*****

In my love dream with Duft, the fierce-smelling edge of our passion is worshipped in dancing fragments of exactly scented stars burst into odorific astonishment: a towering pink collision driven into her slowly until the howling muscles of throttled beauty erupt into a fluttering turbulence, blazing for miles.

29

Silken, moist, dusted with sugar and soft sleep, our new music plays in speechless ecstasy.

Our sensory carousel spins not quite out of control. Neurons in the olfactory center of our brains, clustered near the junction of the parietal and temporal lobes, do the one thing they are programmed to do, with no thought to anything else:

They interpret odors.

Duft's neurons contact me. I absorb her signature scent and pull it inside of me. Duft, in turn, exercises her nasalis muscles by inhaling back into her that which she has already expelled. Once the message is received, her strangely perfect body goes into complete horripilation. And she vibrates.

It doesn't take long. Nerve ends flutter, blood rushes through her veins, the skin becomes flushed, and the specialized cells in her endocrine gland go into overdrive, secreting hormones directly into the bloodstream, seeking out their target: my receptor sites. Duft's hormones lock on, and the resulting electrical impulses stimulate her cells into a beehive of activity. Her serotonin levels fly off the chart and the "humming dance" ensues.

I am the receptacle awaiting Duft's energy. She is my search engine. We feed one another.

I love the taste of Duft's belly first thing in the morning, and the starchy bristle of her tapered linea nigra.

We come from where we started. We go to where we are.

I am finally home.

*****

In the morning, a tribal council is scheduled. With the exception of Holsie, her husband, and Zinaida—who stay up late, watching videos—everyone immediately crashes in their crowded vehicles. They are disenfranchised *and* cranky.

Dewey and the boys somehow manage to come up with yet

another case of cold beer and they are still partying when the sun rises.

Kwame sends Oris Kumke out to start a fire, then follows him to find out what Dewey and Candy are arguing about.

Dewey accuses Candy of being a sexual alcoholic.

According to Candy, Dewey only says that because he is unable to satisfy her.

Dewey responds by saying that's because she's done everyone in the Mexican Army.

Candy's retort is that she's never seen a Mexican built smaller than Dewey.

Dewey says she ought to know, then accuses her of masculating him in public.

Candy accuses him of trying to get his swerve on.

He calls her a nut buster.

She says he is being pretend-naive.

With his manhood now in question, Dewey promises to participate in the next Toughest Man Alive Contest, no matter where it is.

Kwame wastes no time in getting everyone present to sign a document attesting to the fact that they witnessed Dewey's pledge.

Dewey says he is deadly serious. He concludes his argument by telling Candy, "Well, you act like you're Miss All That with those phony fun bags."

"These are real, nimrod," Candy says. "And you know it."

"Yeah. Bought and paid for by the cartel."

And then, to Duft, Dewey says, "*Those* aren't phony fun bags. That outfit really pops."

Fucking idiot.

Dewey looks right through me as if I didn't hear his last crack. "Candy Panties is getting the fuck heebie-jeebies is what it is. Forget her."

"Oh boo hoo," Candy says, pretending to wipe great big baby tears from her eyes.

The group is a wolf pack without its alpha male, lost and confused, with no clear sense of direction. Tourists without a tour guide. Their spiritual center has collapsed.

Someone needs to step up to the plate.

Candy offers to show her breasts to anyone who wants to see them. Stump Sittingdown, Oris Kumke, and a couple of Dewey's boys, take her up on it.

Holsie's husband wheels himself to a window in the R.V. He gets the entire thing on his digital camera, which will later be downloaded onto one of his websites featuring photos of "tiny tops."

Everyone meets at a fast food restaurant to decide what to do over breakfast. Dewey does not show. Seems someone let the air out of all four of his tires.

Dumb ass.

Over pancakes and bacon, Duft is pressured to reveal the second message left by the channeling child. Her handwritten notes reflect verbatim that which was written on the dry-erasure board that day: *ARMAGEDDON PEPPER RANCH COLORADO*

The key that will open the door.

No one who actually witnessed the event is anywhere to be found. The Cure Girl was allegedly at the landing (or the crash, or whatever), as she had told her followers she would be. Immediately afterwards, and before the authorities could arrive, she broadcast an address where she would be giving audiences and healings as a preparatory cleansing for the Big Day. No one knows what that address is, but Holsie's husband has put his feelers out on the Internet and he assures everyone that he will find it out.

In the meantime, everyone agrees to wait patiently for a sign of some kind. Just like before.

Kwame isn't just anybody's fool. He knows he blew it big time and that he's lucky to be allowed to remain with the group. But he feels they are wrong in waiting at the campground. Kwame's instincts tell him they should move into town, assimilate themselves into the populace, and find out if others passed through there who were at the crash site. Surely somebody would have talked about such an event, and perhaps a local or two might have been moved to go to the mass healing. Or at the very least, they might know where it's taking place.

His suggestion is met with derisive stares. He is told to leave it to Holsie's husband, who is not only wired into the net, but also has a short wave radio setup. Sweating out the possibility that the man with no name is going to upstage him, Kwame understands for the first time that this has become a game of one-upmanship.

Kwame decides to make a bold move. He announces at breakfast that he is staying in town, and if others wish to join him, they are welcome.

Stump Sittingdown eyes Candy lasciviously. He will go wherever she does.

Bob Bluitt is low on gas and his funds are limited, so he decides he will stay in town and, if possible, will remain in the cafeteria until they receive their answers.

Dewey tells Kwame he is full of it, that there is nothing in town for any of them. Kwame reminds Dewey of his pledge and informs him that he passed a bar coming into town—the Blue Goose—whose marquee proclaimed it was Fist Fight Friday with Foxy Boxing beginning at midnight.

Dewey, still hammered from his all-nighter, boasts loudly that he will live up to his promise and show Candy what a real man can do in the ring. Candy Chacon waves a twenty-dollar bill in the air, looking for some action. She is betting that Dewey will pee his pants before the fight is stopped.

Kwame wants ten of that. One of Dewey's boys wants the other ten. Candy gives the forty dollars to Martha Sittingdown to hold. (Back in the day, Kwame would have had that responsibility, but who will stand with him now in the center of the fire?)

So without benefit of a quorum vote, it is settled. Every man for himself.

Dewey leaves in search of a liquor store to get primed for his big night.

Bob Bluitt finds out the coffee refills are free, so his mind is made up. He will remain in the café until he is asked to leave.

The Sittingdowns want to find the nearby village that allegedly contains herds of mutant sheep.

Holsie and her husband have not made up their minds, but they are self-contained and can go just about anywhere. Zinaida doesn't care where they go as long as she can bake her bundt cake and watch *Jerry Springer*.

The town is small, and the inhabitants eye the strangers warily. They aren't dressed in camouflage fatigues and nobody drives a pickup truck, and that makes many of the locals suspicious.

As a rule, they are tight-lipped, but the excitement of the past few days has loosened a few lips. Residents are ready to talk.

Kwame sees this as an opportunity to redeem himself. He assigns Oris Kumke the relatively easy task of restocking their cooler and checking the fluids in the car while he interviews select locals about what they may have witnessed or overheard recently.

He strikes pay dirt with Amy Wagenblast, a young artist wannabe stuck in the small town with no way out. She saw the object immediately after it struck the ground and was one of the first on the scene, together with her three brothers, all members of the local militia. She was also present when Beth (the Cure Girl now has a name!) gave directions to her home for the mass healing.

Kwame is giddy with excitement. The group will have to listen to him now. But he must first ensure that Amy talks to no others and that her brothers keep their big yaps shut. He offers to buy her lunch.

But Amy is not hungry. At least not for saturated fats and carbos. She wants to join up with them and start a new life somewhere else on the planet.

"I want to go somewhere. Find a door. Step through it. Close it behind me. Lock it. Give the key to a friend. Or not." This is how Amy sees her future.

Kwame is reluctant to accept responsibility for another tourist, especially one so artsy-fartsy. He decides to string her along, see what information he can glean from her before striking any kind of deal. But he knows he must be very, very clever with this one. He cannot let the others know about her.

Amy makes a pouty face. She puts her little hands on Kwame's head and neck and lifts herself up on her tippy toes. Soft as the breath of a sad butterfly, Amy whispers in Kwame's ear, "Amy needs to be exploited. Amy wants to be used."

Dewey and the boys would be all over this one like white on rice. Kwame mentally puts the kid gloves on.

Kwame is about to tell Amy that she can come with him to get his car when the fickle winds of change, as they are wont to do, shift spontaneously. The roar of a dozen motorcycle engines drown out anything Amy has to say, but Kwame can see by the widening of her big eyes that she is more than just a little excited by the herd of gleaming phallic Harleys.

The collective organism of the group is a living exhibit that changes daily. A work in progress. The dynamic of the members changes continually, and Kwame knows this. So when the Wolfpack (Western Chapter) arrives in town, the weighty pain of change is palpable. Only this time it's like a red-hot poker being pushed up his rectum. And Kwame does not like the feeling at all. His instincts tell him everything he needs to know: the alpha male has arrived.

Kwame protectively puts a hand on Amy's arm, ostensibly to warn her about the potential trouble he envisions, but with nary a glance in his direction, she shakes his hand loose and races towards the group.

"Snake!"

A work in progress.

Step aside.

*****

The gravel parking lot outside the Blue Goose is jam-packed with pickup trucks of every vintage, make and model, most of which sport a gun rack. Kwame counts thirteen chromium Harley-Davidson motorcycles. Crush, Snake's enforcer, guards the bikes, smoking a cigarette and drinking a longneck. Backing him up are two Wolfpack prospects, tattooed and vile looking, black sheep brothers from different mothers.

"I don't like this," Kwame mutters.

"I'm packing heat, just in case things get hinky," Oris Kumke says.

Kwame doesn't like that either. He knows that, as a group, the Wolfpack are nothing more than a professional hit squad. And you don't fuck with people like that.

Dewey's rag-top Pontiac is parked akimbo with the front end nosed into an irrigation ditch.

Holsie and her husband are there. Kwame can see Zinaida inside the R.V., fixing her hair, adjusting her makeup. Holsie's husband stares transfixed at his monitor. Kwame believes he can see naked people cavorting on the computer screen, but he is unsure.

One of Dewey's boys comes around from the side of the building, zipping up his trousers. He waves at Kwame and Oris Kumke.

"Dude. He's totally torn down."

"What?"

"Dewey."

"What about Dewey?"

"Faded. See ya ringside."

"I gotta see this," Kwame says. Oris Kumke follows him inside.

The small pre-fab building is packed with men in Wranglers or camouflage fatigues. Everyone wears a baseball cap with some sort of logo on it. People scream at one another to be heard above the country music that is being played.

What was once a small dance floor has been transformed into a boxing ring. Nylon rope outlines the general shape of the ring. There are two folding chairs at opposite corners.

Kwame searches for a table, but there is nowhere to sit in the hot and humid room.

Amy is seated on Snake's lap. She waves at Kwame. He smiles back. She is wearing a jean jacket vest.

Snake grabs a handful of Amy's hair, pulls her head to him, asks her something. Amy puts her mouth up against Snake's hairy ear and says something back. Snake nods.

Amy stands up and turns around so Kwame can see her vest. The rocker beneath the motorcycle club's logo declares her to be "Property of the Wolfpack (Western Chapter)." She smiles, waves again, then plops back down on Snake's lap. He puts a Camel in his mouth, and waits. Amy lights it for him.

"She's no use to us now," Kwame says.

Oris Kumke shrugs, points to the sign that lets him know the two-for-one beers are only in effect for another thirty minutes.

Duft is on an olfactory high. Her nostrils flare, then go into overdrive, her vibrissae fluttering like a butterfly in heat. Bombarded with the hormonal sex-scent in the room and the pervasive bar stench, her downy body hairs have already reached fully erect status. In this odorized environment of beer, sweat and testosterone, her primary cranial nerve is percolating fairly out of control. She is breathless, and beautiful beyond belief.

Stump Sittingdown is working the room solo. Martha's at

home with Junior, and this is the first night out with the boys Stump has had in a long time. He wants to know where Candy is.

Candy has signed up for the wet t-shirt contest to be held immediately after the first fight. The local girls, many of whom are shapeless and tired looking, eye her with trepidation.

Men with long hair and beards ogle the contestants, making loud and rude comments about their physical attributes. Candy appears to be the hands-down favorite to win the hundred-dollar prize money, although a cross-eyed blonde girl with massive breasts might give her a run for her money.

The plug is pulled on the jukebox.

A rough man dressed in orange coveralls and wearing a baseball cap advertising a local feed store, rattles a large cowbell. Those wanting to test their pugilistic skills are asked to come forward and sign up, bringing with them the twenty-dollar entrance fee.

There will be eight fights in the first elimination round. The winner of each battle will have his name placed into an empty pitcher. The winner of the wet t-shirt contest will have the honor of drawing at random the pairs of names who will fight one another in the next round. The bloodfest will continue until there are two fighters left. Whoever wins that contest will be named the champion and will receive two hundred dollars plus free drinks until closing time. His name will be added to the Fist Fight Friday Hall of Fame board that hangs above the bar.

Once the champion is crowned, Foxy Boxing will begin. There is no entry fee for that contest. Losers of the wet t-shirt competition are encouraged to give it a go. No prize money will be awarded, but the bartender will be liberal with free shots for anyone willing to slip on the oversized Everlasts.

And then it's go time.

Amy applauds Snake, the first to sign up. A slew of regulars, big-boned and corn-fed, pony up their twenties.

There is a brief altercation when other Wolfpack members decide they want to enroll, but time constraints limit the number of entrants, so those still wanting to fight are asked to take it outside. Threats are made and, amid all the posturing, Dewey manages to get signed up.

Oris Kumke pats his thigh. Kwame doesn't get it.

"The Brooklyn Bullwhip. I got it right here."

Kwame can't believe his ears. So now Oris Kumke is armed with *two* weapons.

Dewey makes a point of walking over to Kwame. As much as Kwame would love to see Dewey get his just desserts, he feels it is only fair to issue a warning.

"You are playing a dangerous game."

Dewey blows his boozy breath into Kwame's face. He says, with a snarl, "Yeah? You wanna play games, old man? Put up yer twenty then. Or how 'bout I just punch yer face in right here."

Kwame wants to know why Dewey doesn't like him.

"You gotta be shittin' me, right?" And with that, Dewey staggers up to the bar to be fitted for a pair of gloves. He is surprised to learn that only the foxy boxers will be putting on the Everlasts.

Snake wants Amy to sign up, but she knows better.

"Not with Erline."

"Who's Erline?"

Amy points out the cross-eyed blonde whose cigar-stub nipples have almost punched their way through the synthetic fabric of her overworked t-shirt.

Although a ranch hand at a nearby table describes Erline as "fifty pounds of ugly in a ten-pound sack," Snake is clearly impressed. "Wow," he says.

"Yeah, wow. She wins almost every Friday."

Snake and Dewey are paired up for the first bout.

Snake demands some tongue for luck, and Amy happily obliges.

"Gotta go to work now," Snake says, and climbs into the ring. It doesn't last long.

The cowbell has barely rung before Snake's lethal fists cut into the drunken Dewey. Bones crackle and snap, and flesh pops open. Dewey is exhorted on, but despite the encouragement, he can only submit to the ass-kicking of his life.

Just seconds into the bout, Oris Kumke overstates the obvious. "He's on his last leg."

"His batteries are running down," one of Dewey's boys offers.

"He's drunker than a brewmeister's farts," a big farm hand observes.

"Damn, Sam! Put some fucking *love* into it!" Stump yells.

But Dewey has no love left to give.

"The biker's going Burma on the kid," someone says.

The ringing of the cowbell is only a formality. The punching bag once known as Dewey is out like a light. His boys scamper into the ring.

"Dude. He's twitchin', but. . . ."

"He's perved."

The boys study Dewey closely. A leg shudders. One final spasm, then nothing. Dewey's new address is Dream Street.

"Dude. He's not getting up."

"Passed out?"

"Unconscious."

"Dude."

They eventually get Dewey to his feet.

"Don't forget his teeth," someone yells.

Snake is barely winded. "Give Snake some sugar," he tells his new squeeze. Amy thrusts her tongue into Snake's mouth.

Grinning from ear to ear, Snake tells his pack brothers, "The little guy was actually coming towards me. I had to put him down." Everyone has a good laugh.

Snake raises his arms in victory. The hot room reverberates

with the chant, "Snake! Snake! Snake! Snake!"

Candy can't resist. She confronts the limp Dewey and screams in the face that resembles red popcorn, "You want sympathy? Look in the dictionary, asshole! It's somewhere between 'shit' and 'syphilis'!"

Candy dances with joy, her little breasts rocking and rolling inside her tight t-shirt.

"Check his pants. We got forty big ones riding on this."

One of Dewey's boys tells her he will look, but with one proviso: "I'm not touching him there."

"You won't have to," Candy promises. "You can probably smell it. Pull his pants down!"

Kwame rushes to the ring. He has to see for himself.

"I knew it!" Candy shrieks with uncontrolled jubilation.

Dewey's boys are as shocked as everyone else in the room.

"Dude's wearing panties," one of them says in disbelief.

"Not only that," Candy yells, "but they're designers. Yellow in the front and brown in the back. Pay up!"

Something dawns on Candy that she hadn't thought of before.

"Hey, wait a minute. Those better not be mine."

"They're not," one of the boys confesses. "I was with him when he bought 'em."

The rag doll Dewey regains consciousness in a strange bar packed with drunken ranch hands and bikers. He has a hard time focusing. His teeth are missing, his panties are soiled, and he can actually see his own lips. One eye doesn't work right and he has no idea what happened to his trousers.

Candy wins the wet t-shirt contest after a bizarre and grotesque dance-off with Erline. Flush with success, and primed with 180-proof rum, Candy allows nearly everyone in the bar to do shots off her tummy and ass. Complete strangers stuff her pink thong with dollar bills.

Sometime around 2:00 a.m., Snake knocks a hillbilly named

Luther unconscious with a boot to the temple. Amy is so aroused that she and Snake have sex in the billiard room and again outside against the cinder block wall.

Without looking back, Amy climbs aboard Snake's Indian Spirit Deluxe and the Wolfpack follows them out of town.

It is assumed the distraught Erline kicked everybody's ass and won the Foxy Boxing challenge. Again.

*****

Snake leads the motorcade now. He has given Dewey the nickname Gravy Brains. No one says anything, especially Dewey, benefactor of a lisp and a lazy eye courtesy of Snake's pounding.

Strapped to the back of Snake's machine, Amy guides her man through the treacherous mountain roads, shouting directions in his hairy ears, leading him—and everyone else—to the promised land.

The new order upsets Kwame. Relegated now to mere follower, his pride will not allow him to bring up the rear of the column, so he dangerously passes whomever he can to avoid occupying the last position which, in the past, had been assigned to Holsie Colldren and her husband. But now Snake wants the R.V. closer to him, so everyone must defer to the bigger and slower bus. He has gotten used to eating hot microwaved food whenever his belly is empty, and Zinaida is his literal meal ticket.

Snake announces to the group one night that he thinks Zinaida is hot and that he wants to do her.

"That's just the meth talking," Amy says, and laughs.

Walbert sees nothing funny about this since Zinaida will not feed him, and he seethes inwardly when she refers to him in Snake's presence as "the guy with the bunk spunk."

Walbert complaints to Briola about her mother's newfound confidence—no, arrogance!—and although Briola pretends to listen and act concerned, her thoughts are elsewhere. She wonders what it is like for Amy when Snake takes her roughly, as surely he must. The thought of the two of them locked together in carnal union causes her pulse to race and her ovaries to giggle. She trembles when a strange fluttering tickle pleases her inside.

"The whole thing sickens me," Walbert tells her.

"I know," Briola sighs. "Me too."

Candy Chacon is elated. With money in her pockets and unbridled respect as wet t-shirt champ, she is on cloud nine, despite Dewey's negativity.

"Any dumb ath could have won the fuckin' thing," he lisps.

"Flat on your back with a load of poop in your panties. It's a real surprise you didn't win."

"Neck time we thtop, you're riding with thumb-one elth."

"Fine with me."

Dewey's boys are upset at this breaking news. Candy was awesome company and she was generous with the hand jobs when they partied.

"I mean it," Dewey says. "And anyway, he fuckin' thucker-punked me."

"Guess the judges didn't see that," Candy says, nonplussed.

Everything has changed.

With Snake in charge, the Wolfpack stops at isolated campgrounds and disregard the cheap motels that Kwame had come to enjoy. He expresses his disappointment to Oris Kumke.

"There. You see that?"

"See what." Oris Kumke snaps his Brooklyn Bullwhip against his palm, ready for anything.

"Motel 8. Drove right by it."

"No."

"Second one."

"Didn't see it."

"Are you even looking?"

"Not really."
"Why bother," Kwame mutters.
"With what?"
"I'm not talking to you."
"Well who then."
"Well who then," Kwame mimics.
"I said that," Oris Kumke says.
"I said that," Kwame mimics.
"I said that too."

*****

Duft scratches furiously in her notebook, turning letters into words, words into poetry. She looks up every few moments and inhales deeply, absorbing odor molecules from the air and directing them to her olfactory bulb. Trillions of cells in her brain send millions of messages instantaneously across her synaptic gap, where they are hungrily devoured by neurotransmitters and neurohormones. A lissome gasp, her candy breath escapes in delicious billows, and she continues scribbling in earnest, her minikin fingers curled around the inexpensive ballpoint pen, working in perfect tandem with those cerebral synapses to create the tangled thoughts that will ultimately unravel on lined paper to reveal her startling psyche.

Total functification.

*****

The town is called Straystar. It is where the Cure Girl lives.

No one is certain, but the general consensus is that everyone is back in Colorado.

Amy and Snake have brought us here. But we are not the first. Abandoned vehicles block all roads in and out of the small town.

Cars and vehicles are parked everywhere. Mobile homes and trailers plug up intersections. Tents are pitched in parking lots. Barbecues and hibachis smoke on street corners.

They're all here, stacked up in a holding pattern for the hopeless until they can find somewhere else to land—the sick, maimed, ugly, unfortunate—pop culture gypsies traveling from one overhyped event to another. Tribal members of a tabloid nation, crawling on their hands and knees through the dark dementia of Middle America, and nobody knows where they come from or where they are headed next.

But we are here now. And we want answers.

Kwame is astounded by the sheer numbers. He takes the opportunity to ditch Oris Kumke in the crowds and makes his way solo. What he doesn't know is that the line to see the Cure Girl is already six blocks long. He falls in step with a television crew and follows them towards Beth's house.

Candy Chacon has divorced herself from Dewey and the boys and she wastes no time in hooking up with a hapless CNN reporter who has become separated from his sound man. She agrees to lug the bulky equipment in exchange for a free ride on the coattails of his media credentials.

The Sittingdowns evacuate their vehicle, still running, at a red light a mile away from the city limits. Stump grabs Junior by the neck and they follow the crowd swell into Straystar.

Amy is beside herself. Snake plows through the crowds, his rough hands possessively cupping her tiny waist, while Wolfpack brethren punch out any fool stupid enough to get in their way. There is no doubt they will go directly to the front of the line.

Walbert and Briola have a bitter fight about where to park. They waste precious time arguing about how they will find their vehicle later. Briola carries two liters of bottled water with her, hopeful that the Cure Girl will turn them into Niagara.

Zinaida and Holsie Colldren work as an efficient team, getting

Holsie's man out of the R.V. and into his chair. They both push the wheelchair at breakneck speed, clipping strangers from behind who cannot see them coming.

Bob Bluitt tries to bum a beer from Dewey, but Dewey is in a foul mood and will not share. Bob Bluitt becomes argumentative, accuses Dewey of being selfish.

"Rock on or thuck off, pal," Dewey tells him.

It's almost impossible to get anywhere near the house. Throngs of people surround the Cure Girl's residence. Lines have been formed that now extend for many blocks. The maimed and disfigured patiently wait their turn, but they are not adverse to a physical confrontation should anyone try and cut in line.

A rallying cry from the rear of the house. Reporters rush to see what fresh miracle has taken place.

A once-crippled girl is having her leg braces zealously ripped off by her father. He cries genuine tears of joy.

"My god! Does anybody *know*! Did you people *see* this?"

The father yanks the braces loose and holds them aloft, together with his daughter's crutches, in a triumphant gesture. He rushes off the porch, his young daughter hobbling behind him. They plow through a jubilant crowd, ankle-deep in fast-food debris.

A reporter pulls the girl aside. A camera appears. A microphone is thrust in her face. People touch her legs. Everybody wants to be a part of the macabre miracle.

The neighborhood is in chaotic disorder.

Snake punches his way towards the front of the line. Amy hangs on to his vest for dear life.

A pretty Laotian news reporter clutches her microphone and addresses a camera. "Like the rest of these people, we are here to see Beth. And it's a long line. What you see around you is no Hollywood set, and these are not professional actors. These people are very real. So is Beth Redding. So is what you are about to see."

Handsome Dan from channel 72 quickly combs his hair and moistens his lips.

"Is she possessed? Did a saucer come to Earth from some distant plant and exchange bodies with young Beth Redding? Is that, in fact, really Beth Redding inside the house performing miracles right now? And what about her frightening prediction of Armageddon? What does Beth *really* know? We'll answer these and other questions right after these important words from tonight's sponsors."

Bob Bluitt walks between Handsome Dan and his camera, flashing incomprehensible hand signals into the lens.

Closer to the house, a trendy blonde with fashionable eyeglasses, reads from her script.

"Scam or science? Lunatic or luminary? Fact or fiction? Is Beth Redding a faith healer, or is this just some cruel exploitation gimmick? Does she possess some secret knowledge given to her by another race of people, or is she some modern-day Nostradamus? What else does she know? Where does she get her information? And what is she keeping from us? What *isn't* she saying?"

The sound man wants to do another take.

"This is fucking ridiculous," the blonde bombshell grouses.

Candy offers to do a sound bite for the CNN reporter. She gets it in one take.

"In a way it's like Lourdes. I mean, I've never been there, but, you know, she's healing people and everything. Making predictions. All that stuff." Candy points her perfect little breasts at the camera and smiles. The reporter is pleased.

"We can do another one later if you want," Candy offers. "I'll fix my hair different and put on another top."

But Candy won't have to disguise herself or pretend to be another tourist. Lens lice are everywhere and the competition is fierce for face time on national television.

47

A face peers into a camera. "The energy here crackles! Can you feel it? It's electrical, man." The face disappears.

Another face materializes in front of television screens across the country. "Yo, Shorty!" He gives a shout out to all his peeps. Mad props to everybody back home, and then he's gone. Another blip disappearing off America's radar screen.

The hopelessly addicted and disturbed enter the Cure Girl's residence through the front door, then exit through the rear as newly cured devotees. Each appearance draws a standing ovation from the God-inspired multitude who have turned out for this event.

A media buffet. And it's all you can eat.

And the dark side. You've got to have that. Ain't no party 'til a eye gets put out.

Rumors fly that someone has captured on videotape footage of young Beth in a frantic spasm, strapped to a chair, oblivious to what is happening outside her house and in the yard. Reportedly the tape reveals her thrashing violently, writing on large sheets of newsprint, while her mother rips off page after page and flings them out of the way as fast as she can, exploiting her own sick child.

The frenzy thickens when an angry woman plants herself in front of a camera.

"I'm a neighbor, and I think this should be stopped now! Look at this place! I've called the police time and time again and they won't do a thing! My god, there is a young girl in that house having seizures and carrying on who should be institutionalized! People from all over come here now, day and night, because they've been sold a bill of goods that she's some kind of oracle! Well, she's not any of that!"

When asked how else to explain all the healings that have taken place, she responds, "The healings? How would I know! Luck, I guess!"

Dewey and the boys (sans Candelaria Chacon) make their way inside the front gate. They boldly attempt to cheat their way through a small encampment of cripples. Immediately an indignant cry goes up and they are soundly beaten back. There will be no line cuts. No free passes.

But the real cherry is this: During the massive public healings, Beth has also managed to pinpoint where people are to go to avoid the rapidly approaching millennium disaster.

One local television news team captures it this way:

Patricia, perfectly coiffed and capable anchorwoman, furrows her brow. "And if you think this is bad, wait until you see Scott McMurphy, our on-the-spot western bureau correspondent, at the Pepper Ranch in the Colorado Rockies. Scott?"

Scott is launching his exclusive remote from the actual Pepper Ranch.

"Thanks, Patricia. We are high in the Colorado Rocky Mountains, surrounded by pine, blue spruce, aspen, and mountain peaks that seem to, well, touch the heavens. A peaceful place. Thousands and thousands of acres of open grazing and ranch land, surrounded by towering snow-capped peaks. Miles away form civilization. Ah, Wilderness! This is *the* place to get away from it all. Shangri-La. . . ."

The camera pans. Millions of viewers are treated to an endless caravan of motorbikes, cars, trucks, jeeps, campers and vans, all streaming onto Pepper Ranch, completely devastating the fragile mountain ecology.

A ragged trail of backpackers trek off on their own, ant-like, into the mountains.

Scott McMurphy is serious about what he is seeing with his own two eyes: "...that is until some little girl said the world was going to come to an end in some apocalyptic manner and that only those who came here to Pepper Ranch would be saved. Well, they are coming. And coming. And how will they be saved? Well, it seems that a gigantic spaceship is going to come down here and take everybody away—this, according to Beth—away to a place where, who knows, maybe there's a busload of people waiting to come here. Patricia? Back to you."

His delivery is sufficiently powerful enough to keep most of the nation on the edge of their seats.

Patricia fires back:

"Thank you, Scott. And you be careful of the scalpers. I understand you just paid double the going rate for a one-way ticket to Moon City."

Everyone in the studio laughs. The sound waves are picked up by millions of ears in millions of homes where millions of people entertain themselves with the spontaneous bon mots they have come to expect from the attractive news team.

But Scott is caught off guard. He looks confused and insecure. He adjusts his ear mike, but no one is telling him what to say. He has no words. He is unable to improvise and he comes off looking like an idiot, staring blankly into the monitor. He smiles his Emmy winning smile, but viewers will comment the following day that he appeared to be in a tremendous amount of pain.

America watches in fascination the tableau that is unfolding before their candied junky eyes.

The suburban insanity spikes when out of nowhere Bob Bluitt appears amid a group of crippled and wounded, pretending to be lame. Feeble and impotent fists flail away at him when his ruse is discovered. Unable to convince the angry votaries that he is one of them, Bob Bluitt impulsively stuffs all the money he has into the hands of a startled and confused mother, scoops her disabled child up in his arms, and once again heads for the house.

Cradling the youngster like a living backstage pass, Bob Bluitt rushes the front door, but is repelled again by those angered at the thought of giving up their place in line. Frustrated and angry, he drops the child into the chaotic mob and makes a run for his own life.

Step aside.

As if on cue, the crowd begins to part.

The monster of a man who will carry the sobriquet "Assassin" from this day forward, appears. He walks past the perimeter of the house, shoving helpless people out of his way.

When the assassin tries to force his way through a screen door on the side of the house, the infuriated legions charge him.

With an eerie and deliberate calm, the assassin assumes the stance of a professional killer, his large handgun leveled at the mob.

Undaunted, a crippled man slams a metal crutch into the assassin's head. The big man drops, and the gun goes off. The errant slug seeks out an unsuspecting Brahulyo Saucedo and instantly drains the life from him. When the mob gets its collective breath back, it viciously turns on the assassin and rips him from limb to limb.

Someone carries Brahulyo's corpse to the front of the line. Others scoop up the remains of The Assassin and follow. Out of respect, an exception is made; the crowds part and they are allowed to pass and enter the house ahead of everyone else.

Less than an hour later the once-dead Brahulyo Saucedo and the assassin miraculously appear in the doorway, bloodied and shaken, but otherwise perfectly fine. They receive a standing ovation. Drained, the assassin puts his arm around the man he murdered only moments before and, like two long-lost brothers, they help each other back inside the house.

Brahulyo Saucedo, seeking contrition, has found forgiveness and becomes whole. Once the pilot of a 20-ton missile that snuffed out a life, he now restores life, this time as a peace-loving mystic. Brahulyo Saucedo is a saint. He touches and heals.

Bob Bluitt christens this a movin' metallic night, slaughtered with sparklers. He says he has gum jaw, gets the jaw jumpers. Sticky eyes. He keeps calling everything sky slaughter. Others will claim he was scared shitless and the experience forever changed his demeanor.

"It's a movin' metallic night," he will say to anyone. "Do you feel it?" When they attempt a response, he cuts them off with, "Don't say it, you'll ruin everything."

Bob Bluitt is different somehow.

The event is documented from every aspect and angle possible. The media coverage ratchets up a notch or two, luring more and more curious to the site.

The almighty dollar barks and scalpers answer the call.

Someone starts taking money, selling tickets. It is every man, woman and child, for themselves.

Holsie Colldren and her man have been given special dispensation because of his chair and they are ushered in quickly. When they exit from the rear of the house almost two hours later, Holsie proudly pushes her husband, who punches a triumphant fist into the air.

"We got what we came for! Carpal's gone!"

Expert pickpockets work the confused mobs effortlessly, gliding from one unsuspecting mark to another. Many people just *give* their money away. Even more miracles.

Every sickness and disease you can think of; every malady and disorder known to exist. And then some.

A new obstacle presents itself. As soon as someone is healed, they pour out onto the streets, anxious to begin their journey to the Pepper Ranch. More people are leaving than are arriving.

Complete chaos. Traffic at a complete stop. Gridlock beyond comprehension.

There is little to eat.

New, healthy bodies begin to outnumber the broken, bruised and dismembered army of the unwell.

Move and touch. Touch and move.

Make a place for another.

Briola submits to a laying of the hands and leaves the house feeling flushed, refreshed, and very light on her feet. She will patiently await the promised miracle, but until that happens, she will nurse the two liters of precious fluid blessed by Beth.

Walbert's wish had unfortunately already come true when he got rid of Zinaida, but now he wants her back. It is not the same without her. He is hungry and Briola will not cook. Walbert wants to go back to Spanish Pork, and he wants Zinaida to go with them. But he is wary of Snake's newfound interest in Zinaida and he fears that Snake will make his move soon and she will be lost forever. If he has to, Walbert says he will buy Zinaida back.

Briola could care less. She dreams of the frenzied activity taking place inside of her, the electrically charged awakening she has waited her entire life for.

Kwame does a double take when he runs into Dewey. His orthodontics are flawless and there is no trace of the dozens of stitches that only hours before criss-crossed the inside of his swollen, purple lips. His sluggish left eye is alert and no longer bloodshot. Dewey has been repaired.

Kwame is truly stunned. "Gravy Brains? That you?"

Dewey looks like a million bucks. Just a little more evil.

"Chew my bag," Dewey says, and pushes his way through the crowd.

It's Dewey all right. The malignant attitude remains unchanged.

And so it goes. One by one the sea of people parade through the house. No one gets left behind.

Darkness descends on the tiny hamlet. Dozens of bonfires contribute to the surreal landscape, illuminating the wreckage left behind. The masses have expressed their gratitude by trashing the town and leaving behind tons of acrid fecal matter.

Uniformed and plainclothes police officers question hundreds of people about a killing that allegedly took place. Nobody knows what they are talking about.

*****

Snake has never really wanted anything in life other than true love. Desperate for the nurturing love of an older woman—his mother—his fondness for Zinaida has become primal and obsessive. He does not think he can go on without her.

At the Appreciation for Beth Bonfire that night, Snake puts his arms around Zinaida. Hungry for the touch of another person, she falls easily against him. Encouraged, Snake splays his hands over her ample hips. He pulls her blouse free, glides his hands beneath the polyester fabric. He runs his engine-oiled fingers over her flesh, up her back to her lumpy shoulders and around to her jellied belly. Aroused like he's never been before, Snake cups Zinaida's pendulous breasts lovingly in his unsmooth hands.

"Mommy," he says, with closed eyes, his voice barely a whisper.

Zinaida quivers uncontrollably.

Break out the Buffalo wings.

None of this fazes Amy, who continues to work the crowd like a pro. She will make it to the Final Day of Annihilation no matter what. If she wants to. She may go to California or New York instead. Or not. It doesn't really matter. Beth has bestowed upon Amy the gift of poetry and songwriting and she can now create her art anywhere.

When she sees Snake clinging to Zinaida, she asks him if he is slamming trash cans now. (Even Amy has to smile. She never could have thought up such a clever putdown before.) Snake can only stare at her with tears in his eyes. Amy takes out her frustration by writing a song about Snake called "Erasable You."

"We are so through," she tells Snake. But Amy doesn't really care. She will have to find a new ride and her sights are now aimed at somebody with a set of wheels—a man who understands art.

Duft.

Duft, Duft, Duft.

She too is cured—no, *transmuted.*

The beauty of her gift has turned on itself.

Hypersensitive now to pesticide residues, concentrated protein, saturated fat, DES and the female sex hormones systematically administered to cattle, Duft stops eating meat and weans herself off all dairy products. Like that! When prompted, she rattles off a laundry list of the evils of milk. It has become her mantra.

Where's the beef? Not in Duft.

Got milk? Duft don't.

With the devotion of a penitent, Duft turns organic and becomes "green"; the colors in my food come from a laboratory filled with chemicals no one can pronounce.

When I try to argue the merits of red meat or dairy, Duft frowns and tells me to expect breasts bigger than hers in ten years.

Beth has somehow managed to eliminate from Duft's beautiful and perfect little temple the horrors of ovarian tumors, cysts, and vaginal infections. Duft embraces this new world where uterine fibroids are a thing of the past. Her skin overnight becomes silky smooth and poreless. Her breath is candy sweet and mysteriously scented, while I age horribly and my body breaks down.

With Duft now at arm's length, the confused receptor sites in my brain continue to beg for synthetic stimulation from chemicals, so I sneak ice cream, disregard the mucous-producing qualities of cheese, and gorge on empty calories wherever and whenever I can find them.

The brand of ice cream I favor is laced with propylene glycol, an antifreeze. I eat gallons of it.

The additives I ingest contain petroleum products that my body will never be able to digest. Many of the chemicals in the food products I crave are associated with cancer.

I devour red meat, pork byproducts. I harbor bovine and porcine DNA within my own cells. Aluminum-containing preservatives? Mmmm. A mind-numbing smorgasbord of non-nutritional items completely devoid of vitamins and minerals. I eat the parts of a pig that a pig won't eat.

I am on a high-fat, high-phosphorous diet.

More sugar, please.

Artificial ingredients, such as MSG and aspartame (so critical to my dietary regime), produce massive amounts of the excitotoxin chemical in my brain, causing it to become overexcited and to fire uncontrollably. My blood-sugar spikes out of control, then plunges to dangerously low levels.

I am a walking, talking, cancer time bomb. But I'm giddy and enthusiastic.

Duft's assessment of my life from this day forward—thinning bones, allergies, headaches, gas, flatulence, hemorrhoids, halitosis, impotence, prostate cancer, Multiple Sclerosis, and, somewhere down the road, a bizarre assortment of sexual aberrations too numerous to mention. She wants nothing to do with someone whose decadent lifestyle is spinning so dramatically out of control. In her eyes I am weak.

My insides churn with a newfound rancor never before imagined. My pheromones come a knockin', but Duft is not at home.

When I try to kiss Duft, she pulls away. She can taste aluminum and trace minerals. She says kissing me is icky. She can't rinse the taste of copper from her mouth. She gargles with hydrogen peroxide.

Shovel to the face.

My aura frightens Duft, and she does not like to be alone with me. Duft's muff for me now is nothing more than a sentimental journey.

I beg to see Beth, determined to have this curse removed from my head. But my pleas go unheard. The little bitch is too exhausted to see any more people and, to move the people through more efficiently, she is refusing to see those whom she considers to be pagan.

My pheromones will have to drift endlessly in the ether, and wobble, unfettered, on the deadened waves of Duftless air.

My television is broken.

*****

Like the tabloids, none of this is real. Smoke and mirrors. Superlatives and accolades; hyperbole. People only see what they want to see, and many see nothing at all. The Virgin Mary never reappears at the appointed hour. Fry up a few billion tortillas and one of them is bound to bear the likeness of Christ. And Elvis has always just left the 7-Eleven by the time you get there.

The worst of the worst, and the group responds with typical pack mentality one-upmanship:.

I have a friend who had a friend who....

My sister dated a guy who knew someone who....

I used to work with somebody who....

Complete me. Make me whole. Take me out of my skin. I want to breathe.

Share what you know. Impart your knowledge unto me.

Let me be you for one moment.

Everyone going for the cure, the change. The new and improved me. The healthy me. The sane me.

Fix me. Change me. Make me real.

I want to be different: Like you.

Sycophantic losers.

I regroup and plot revenge. I will no longer follow the freaks. I will become the freak. And they will follow me.

Time for the deeds to speak for themselves.

I am superior and understand for the first time in my life why I have no friends: Some people are just born lucky.

*****

The Beth Bonfire (why aren't we burning *her!*) brings few surprises. The bongo monkeys (Dewey and his boys) act out as usual, anxious to get back on the road. Only there is no road, just one gigantic parking lot, and until that mess can be straightened out, nobody is going anywhere.

Hence the tribute to Beth, though I don't know why. What exactly has she done, other than assume the role of a modern-day snake oil salesman, giving false hope to thousands of needy nobodies, doling out empty promises to an army of hopeless and lost souls, pathetically desperate for validation. Co-dependency at its worst. She's got her own agenda, trust me. I just don't know what it is.

Another great unknown is exactly when the big annihilation is coming. Current ETA is "fairly soon" (guess it was too difficult for Beth to come up with an actual date), so everyone is in less-than-panic mode, and the tribute begins to resemble a big Fourth of July cookout, except there is precious little food to grill. Like the signs say, "Party like there's no tomorrow! 'Cause there ain't gonna be one!"

I, however, am able to restrain my enthusiasm for this little trickster.

Dewey continues to amaze. He has once again beaten the odds by somehow coming up with several two-liter jugs of vodka and whiskey, in spite of the fact that the police have forced local liquor stores to close their doors. When Kwame questions him, Dewey tells him to sit on his face.

The true miracle is that most members of the group have managed to find one another at all. With some weird kind of homing pigeon instinct, they have managed to reunite once again, finding comfort in the only safe haven they will ever know—in the shared hallucination of the group's dysfunctional brethren.

Candelaria Chacon has resurfaced with Tetsuko Kendo, an aspiring comic who came to see the cure turd seeking fresh material for his standup act. Tetsuko does observational humor and thought this would be a good place to get ideas. His claim to fame is that he was thrown off *Letterman* for making fun of Dave's b.o. Tetsuko insists the *Letterman* people have not heard the last of him. "He has hell to pay for that one."

Tetsuko drives a Lexus, and that little nugget of news is not lost on Candy.

Dewey builds a screwdriver for Tetsuko and tells him, "Candy has that sexual alcoholism, or whatever you call it."

"No shit?"

"Pure, dude."

"Didn't know that," Tetsuko says.

"Square bidness. I ought to know." Dewey winks, then thumps his head as if it was a cantaloupe. "Crazy in the head, crazy in the bed. Know what I mean?"

Tetsuko does not know what he means.

"So tell me a joke."

"I don't do jokes," Tetsuko says.

"Let's see. A comedian that doesn't tell jokes. Shit, dude, no wonder you're not working." Dewey disappears through the crowd. He is selling shots for two bucks.

Amy, still smarting from her breakup with Snake, confides in whomever will listen that she is thinking about going back home, hoping to share in a cash settlement her sister is expected to receive from the airlines and the federal government. Fifteen years ago the government created a deodorant to spray in airplanes to calm nervous passengers. Her sister was a flight attendant for one of the major airlines and was exposed to it for years on a daily basis. The chemicals allegedly made her go crazy, and she's suing. Fearful of terrorists with gas masks, she informs everyone that the government has now concocted an even deadlier spray that enters through the pores. Punitive damages are expected to be in the billions.

Duft is enthralled with Amy's story. The neurons dance crazy in her brain and her downy body hairs rise up in unbridled excitation.

But Amy is not to be pitied. Free from Snake, her creativity soars, and she discusses with Duft an idea she has about changing her name.

"What's wrong with Amy?" Duft wants to know.

"Not Amy. Wagenblast."

"Wagenblast? God yes. To what?"

"Just Blast. A Blast."

"It's a start," Duft says, supplying Amy with the encouragement she was hoping she would find with her new best friend.

Emboldened by Duft's support, Amy (A Blast) performs a capella the songs that have sprung from the creativity of her new soul.

Her inaugural set: "Glad Willow/Sad Willow," "Erasable You," "Breeder Town USA," "Monkey in the Bank," "Playoff Suicide," "Dreamthink," "Stinky One," "No More's Utopia," "Blue, Dog Gone," and "Little Hairy One" (this brought everyone to their feet). She decided not to do "Snake in the Glass" because she didn't think she would be able to get through it.

But the reality is that Snake could give two craps about Amy (or A Blast). He's got Zinaida now. Snake lives now with a constant erection and he thinks of nothing other than becoming lost among Zinaida's soft, fleshy folds. He wants to be smothered by her love. (During Amy's one-woman show at the campfire, Snake held Zinaida, pinned against a blue spruce, rocking and rolling her nipples between his tobacco-stained fingers, awakening from dormancy the erotogenic carnival within her.)

And make no bones about it, Zinaida is a gamer. She has taken to putting drops of vanilla behind her ears and between her breasts because it takes Snake back to the innocence of his childhood, reminding him of the aroma of his mother's freshly baked cookies.

Walbert, mindless with grief and riddled with guilt, has a hunger of his own. Briola is so fixated upon her precious Niagara, which she sips at continually, that she has no interest in preparing even the simplest of meals. With Zinaida out of the picture, the triumvirate is incomplete, and Walbert rehearses plan after plan in his head to lure her back into the family.

Guilt, the great equalizer, has given Walbert a newfound energy to dwell on his actions of the past. He vows he will never again take Zinaida for granted and will do everything in his power to get her back. But money (the other great equalizer) is something Walbert does not have. He hates himself for tipping his hand when he told Snake he would buy Zinaida back if he had to. Walbert knows that if Zinaida will not come back to him of her own volition, he will have to come up with an amount of cash that Snake cannot possibly refuse. Walbert desperately needs bank.

Walbert asks Dewey for his empty vodka bottles. His plan is to fill them with tap water and sell them to unsuspecting rubes looking for a catholicon, made possible by the hands-on blessing from the cure turd. Everyone will have to believe in the curative he hawks because they have seen Beth at work and will know the elixir is the real McCoy.

But Dewey can smell the desperation oozing from Walbert's every pore and he demands five bucks for each empty. When Walbert balks at the price and suggests that Dewey consider it a charitable act, Dewey tells him to slob on his knob. He shatters the empties in front of Walbert and tells him he ought to be using any available water to do something about "all that sweat and pissperation."

For Walbert, this is just another reality slap on his already reddened ass. He wracks his brain for another plan.

Bob Bluitt announces in front of the now-roaring bonfire that it is going to be another movin' metallic night and to expect something boom-bad, and soon. Very soon. He is unfazed when Duft, Amy, and Candy, decline his offer to enlist in his sub Barbie Army.

Oris Kumke has somehow ingratiated himself to Holsie Colldren. He has stopped taking his medication—he has no money and can no longer afford the luxury of antidepressants—and this sends him into full assault mode. So with perfect vision now and zero self-control, he is about as dangerous as they come. Holsie pities him.

Not Duft. She suggests he get on a regimen of high-dose L-tryptophan, which is as good a tranquilizer as Valium, and no prescription is required.

In spite of the dark skies and the rules forbidding night fishing, Oris Kumke pledges to everyone that he will supply fresh fish for an old-fashioned fish fry. Holsie rummages through the R.V. and produces several rods and reels. Holsie's old man tells her to make sure that anyone borrowing one of his poles signs out for it and that it is returned the next day.

Kwame mocks Oris Kumke. "What about bait?"

"Don't need it here," Oris Kumke tells him. "All the trout have that twirling disease. They just spin and spin and spin. Just wade in and scoop 'em up."

Amy and Duft both chime in: "Gross."

"They want to be caught," Oris Kumke explains. "There's nothing wrong with them. They have no mind left, that's all."

Amy insists the trout do not want to be caught.

"This is Colorado, baby," Dewey tells her. "Eye of the storm.

Zen center of the West. All the fish are like that."

Amy takes a stand. "I'm not eating them."

"Yeah? Well, here's another news flash for ya. All the deer and elk you've been seeing? Every single one of 'em is inflicted with Chronic Wasting Disease." Dewey laughs. "Ever hear of it? Eats holes in their brains. One step away from Mad Cow Disease. Think about that next time you order up a burger."

"We don't eat meat," Duft says.

"Yeah," Amy chimes in. "So there."

"Then have fun fillin' up on air biscuits." Dewey grabs a pole. "Oh, and one other thing. Highest rate of skin cancer and prostate cancer on the planet—right here."

"It's the brown cloud," Oris Kumke tells them. "The thin air." And he ought to know, he's a native.

"And the water," Dewey adds.

"What are we supposed to drink then?" someone wants to know.

"Not this!" Briola clutches her precious Niagara to her bosom.

Dewey promises everyone he will sponsor a happy hour when they return—screwdrivers or straight-up vodka shots. Three bucks a pop.

Dewey, Oris Kumke, Crush, and a few soldiers from the Wolfpack, troop off into the night, in search of the nearest non-polluted creek or river.

When they are out of earshot, Holsie blurts out that she has been secretly sitting on a 32-ounce sack of popcorn, but when Duft sees it is to be popped in an aluminum pan, she declines. Amy follows suit.

A boom box is set up and Snake and Zinaida slow dance around the blazing fire.

Duft is holding court. We've heard it a million times: When good enzymes go bad. Colonic irrigation this, colonic irritation that. Everyone's familiar with the party line by now. Even the

Sittingdowns, who sit side by side in matching plastic lawn chairs, both of them fussing with baby Sittingdown, now wrapped in a t-shirt bearing the likeness of the little goddess bitch who ruined everything, and the quote, "My parents went to see the Cure Girl and all I got was this lousy shirt."

All I got was shit.

Depression and neurological dysfunction. Blah blah blah. Cramps and constipation. Blah blah. Sodium lactate and panic attacks. Blah.

This is not the eye of the storm. The only thing we are in the middle of is the lunatic fringe.

Gone tabloid. Every single one of them.

Kwame is silent and morose. He picks at his freshly popped corn, each kernel a biting reminder of the moment when it all went south on him—the corn maze in Nebraska.

Kwame needs a big event. A decisive act or incident that will turn everything around and get them back on track. Kwame itches to be back in control again. He checks his Nokia for messages. There are none.

The fishing expedition can only be considered a failure. Back in camp barely an hour after leaving, it's obvious something went down. Dewey, soaked from head to toe, grumbles that the others tried to colostomize him. Nobody knows what that means.

Holsie Colldren greets everyone enthusiastically. The iron fry pans have been sitting on hot coals and are ready for the catch. The only catch is there are just three trout, each one smaller than the other. Undaunted, she and Zinaida clean and prepare the trout, dredging them in cornmeal and dropping them in sizzling fat.

The smell sickens Duft, and she moves upwind of the fire to escape the stinging smoke. Amy follows her.

"How was it?" someone asks.

"Don't even," Dewey warns. "Let's just say there are contenders and there are pretenders. We can leave it at that."

Crush issues a warning of his own. "It's gonna get busy around here."

Kwame grins an evil grin. "What happened?"

"If you would'a come fishing with us, then maybe you'd know," Dewey says, and steps up to the fire to dry off.

Oris Kumke clutches a paper plate, a plastic fork, and a Styrofoam cup. "Let's start the happy hour."

"Happy hour this, dickweed," Dewey snarls.

"That's not very righteous," Oris Kumke tells him.

Martha asks Stump what happened and he waves a disgusted hand at her. "Later. How's Junior?"

"He missed his daddy."

The Wolfpack soldiers have nothing to say to the civilians. They trudge off together somewhere beyond the perimeter of the fire, where their bikes are parked and their brothers are waiting. Zinaida follows them. Walbert can't bear to look.

"Do you believe those fucking guys?" Dewey asks rhetorically.

"What did I predicate. Boom-bad sky slaughter. Told ya." Bob Bluitt nods knowingly. Everyone looks at one another.

A camera crew sets up near the fire and begins taping. To the viewers it will appear as if the Bonfire for Beth is a huge success. Later, in the editing room, a voice-over will be used to affirm that illusion.

"Do something," a field producer urges. "Try and look like you're having fun."

Holsie Colldren leans in close to her fry pan, smiling and wafting the fumes towards her face. She is spattered with hot oil and pulls away before they can get the shot.

"Come on, people," the field producer cajoles. "This is your big chance to be on television."

Dewey steps up to the batter's box.

"Want to know what wads my panties?"

"No, we don't want to know," Kwame says. "Why the hell don't you wear boxers like everyone else?"

"'Cause they don't fit me right, that's why. These are snugger. I like that."

"Fuckin' she-male," somebody says.

The camera crew abruptly takes down their setup.

"Thanks, people."

"For what." Dewey glares at them. "Where you going? Can't handle the truth?"

From the dark, the booming voice of Snake.

"Shut the fuck up, Gravy Brains, or we're gonna rumble."

Dewey has to get the last word in. "Rumble this."

"We heard that," Zinaida calls out.

"Yeah, give it a rest, will you?" Candy is seated between Tetsuko Kendo's legs, her back snuggled up against his warm chest. His hands can't be seen, but it's assumed they are somewhere under Candy's shirt.

Dewey wastes no time in accusing Candy of pulling a 360 on him.

"You weren't all that," Candy shoots back.

"What, I didn't bone you good enough? I gave up my mind for you," Dewey responds.

"Then you didn't lose anything."

"Got that right," Dewey snaps back at her, then realizes how stupid he sounds. He will later blame the dumbass remark on his attention deficit disorder. "Anyway, why don't the two of you just go on back to West Pennsyltucky, or wherever the hell you came from."

Dewey changes his voice to a falsetto, mimicking Candelaria. "Ooh, I want the big meat hook. But how much chunk are you gonna spend on me first? Ooh, me so ho'ny!"

The boys laugh, not knowing what else to do.

But Kwame has had enough. "I'm sitting here not believing

this incendiary talk I'm hearing. What is the *matter* with all of you? What happened out there?"

"Nothing! Nothing happened, all right?" Dewey will not talk about it.

"These fish look funny," Holsie Colldren says, poking at the fried trout with a spatula.

"Then don't eat any," Dewey says. "There's not enough to go around anyway."

"Cook the damn things yourself if you're not gonna share." Stung by Dewey's words, Holsie gets up and walks away.

Dewey doesn't know what to do. Unless someone acts quickly, the fish will overcook and burn in the hot fry pan, and Dewey wants to get his grub on.

"They look done to me," he says, not knowing what cooked fish are supposed to look like.

Nobody makes a move, so the boys crowd around the sizzling fish, eager to get some hot food in their bellies.

Oris Kumke steps up with his plate. "I helped too. Give me one of them trout."

"Give you a trouser trout is what I ought to give you," Dewey says, and the boys laugh loudly.

"Yeah, it'll go good with your red snapper," someone suggests.

Oris Kumke pushes his plate at Dewey, unfazed.

Dewey reluctantly cuts the three trout into six fillets. The boys and Oris Kumke devour them all.

The others watch them eat. Like trained circus monkeys on display, Dewey and the boys (and Oris Kumke) pick through the flaky flesh, hopping about on their haunches, yanking out tiny trout bones, grunting and groaning as they devour the white meat.

In minutes the fish are gone. Dewey licks his fingers and throws his plasticware into the fire.

"Now, I know I promised everybody a happy hour after the fish fry…but since the Jack is gone…" He throws an accusatory look in the direction of the Wolfpack camp. "We'll have to make do with vodka only. Or beer. Four bucks each. Furnish your own cup."

Despite the sad and extreme dislike for themselves, the guilt about their innumerable past failures, and their hopeless futures, they are on their way to total functification.

Everyone getting jiggy with something.

Snake, for once, is happy. He doesn't have a clue that his chain smoking is suppressing his immune system to such a degree that each cigarette he ingests destroys 25 mg. of the vitamin C in his body. Not to mention the fact that the two-pack-a-day habit is also robbing Zinaida of 10 mg. of her vitamin C with the deadly second-hand smoke he so arrogantly produces. Snake's diet of methamphetamine, beer and whiskey, polishes off most of his B vitamins, zinc, selenium, vitamin E, and whatever's left of his vitamin C reserve. Even if he quits drinking, the chemicals in the tap water rob what's left of his body's supply of antioxidant micronutrients.

And Candelaria Chacon, she's probably on the pill, putting herself at risk for abnormal clotting, circulatory distress, blood pressure problems and vaginal yeast infections. But, hey, her cycle is regulated and she's a white-hot comet of sexuality. She can fuck like a bunny whenever she wants.

The pallor and wan, lost look on the faces of everyone suggests at least one potentially serious vitamin or mineral deficiency in each of them. The degree of toxemia varies, but everyone here has at least five grams of stored toxins in their body. *At least* five grams.

They slam their canned soda pops, oblivious to the damage the phosphoric acid is doing to them. Each can they guzzle contains nine teaspoons of sugar, enough to compromise what's left of their immune system for the next 12 hours, not to mention the leached aluminum that dive-bombs into their cells. These soda drinkers, if they don't already have Alzheimer's and dementia, will most certainly get it.

And unless Kwame infuses himself with mega doses of biotin, inositol and zinc, he can say goodbye to the rest of his hair.

I deteriorate as rapidly as anyone else.

Our bodies are incapable of deactivating the toxic chemicals permanently stored in our muscle and fat cells. In time, these xenobiotics will cause cellular damage which, in turn, will trigger tissue damage, lighting the fuse for the cancer bomb, heart disease, and immunodeficiency diseases.

Like vigilantes on a mission, free radicals seek out the vulnerable weak cells and, at the very least, the oxidizing effects of all the tissue damage speeds up the aging process. And if you have been paying any attention at all to Duft, you would know that free radicals do the devil's work—they wreak havoc on unwary cells.

The revolution goes in inside of every one of us 24/7. Free radicals destroy the chemical components of our cells, killing many of them outright. The collagen structure in our skin breaks down, and we are left with wrinkles. Muscles wilt, broken bones stay broken, kidneys lose their efficiency, and memory becomes a thing of the past.

But that's only the beginning. If the free radicals make it to the DNA within the cell's nucleus, it's Armageddon time. Once the delicate DNA bonds are broken, the genetic code is altered and the cells begin to mutate, and these genetic mutations are lethal to the cells.

The surviving cells don't fare much better. They become cancerous.

Free radicals contribute to the formation of thick deposits of arterial plaque and, you get enough plaque in your blood vessels, you cut off the supply of oxygen to the heart muscle. When that happens—boom, boom, out goes the light.

I'm a walking, talking, living compost heap, while Duft's porcelain skin becomes more pliant by the minute.

The shiznit.

No diggity, dude.

Denied access to Duft's once-compatible cells, my homeless hormones are now manically flushed through my bloodstream with no place to download their chemical signals. My traitorous receptor sites have no choice but to indiscriminately respond to chemicals produced outside the body, causing a misfiring of the brain's signals, leaving me even more vulnerable to a host of predatory influences, triggering a yard sale of natural opiates in my brain—*endorphins*.

Help yourself. I have more than enough ethyl formate, sodium lactate, sorbic acid, fumaric acid, aspartame, sodium benzoate, acetone peroxide, petroleum naphtha, BHA, BHT, EDTA, TBHQ, yellow dye #5, red dye #40, and aluminum ammonium sulfate. Free for the taking.

Lucy, I'm home!

*****

Zinaida is comfortable in the small biker camp. Camp life agrees with her, in spite of the numerous ticks she finds wedged between her body's folds and pleats. Snake is good to her and she hasn't had a man touch her in 25 years the way Snake does. They have had sex on three occasions, and each time Snake has rocked her world. After Snake erupts inside of her, he quivers and shakes, then cries like a baby and kisses her face and hair and calls her Mommy. Zinaida loves this.

Snake climbs out of their sleeping bag, his smile accompanied by a joyous erection. "I'm gonna go get us a couple of cold ones."

"Not for me, Snake," Zinaida tells him.

"No, for me."

Snake boldly walks in the direction of Gravy Brain's beer stash.

Crush, pissing behind somebody's tent, zips up in front of Zinaida.

"Are you Snake's old lady now?"

"I think so."

"Welcome to the family. You're gonna have to show me your tits, you know."

"I know, Snake told me I have to show everybody. Tell me when."

A nearby sound catches their attention. It is Stump Sittingdown, lurking in the shadows.

"Club members only, dude," Crush tells him.

"Just looking for something," Stump says.

"Look somewhere else."

"Okay." Stump disappears.

Crush has that look in his eyes when he talks to Zinaida. He adjusts his package, then leaves.

Zinaida wanted to look. She just didn't think it proper to sneak a peek at a guy's junk, particularly someone as rough-looking as Crush, with his ponytail and faded Sturgis t-shirt spattered with beer and piss stains.

Zinaida smiles benignly and waves. "'Night, Crush."

Crush grunts. He wants to get back on the road, find a place to settle down so he can cook. The meth stash is being depleted at an alarming rate and he needs time and materials to cook up another batch. He is also concerned about the grenades stashed in his saddlebags, and the Tommy gun planted inside Holsie Colldren's R.V. But this is old hat for Crush. He knows that if she gets popped for possession of his illegal weapons, that's on Holsie and her old man, and Crush is on his way to another rodeo.

It is a warm night. Everyone will sleep under the stars, close to the glowing embers from the huge bonfire. Happy little buddy-lumps scattered everywhere.

Like the lure of the tormenting siren song, I am drawn to the fragrant tumescence of Duft's sleeping body. In dark silence I can only watch.

A few steps closer and I can almost touch the root of her nose, swollen looking, the fleshiness rounding out the alar groove in such a way as to create an almost perfect almond-shaped naris (through which the hypnotic thrush of her soft inhalations and exhalations are almost too much to bear), the tiny cleft of her philtrum made even more startling by the shadows highlighting her philtral ridges.

Beneath Duft's poochy little tummy, amino acids and enzymes continue to churn and gurgle, except now they communicate in a secret language she is no longer willing to share with me. My chemical particles (odors), once blissfully dissolved in the mucous membrane lining of Duft's precious nasal cavity, will never again reach her cranial nerve, or be hosted by her brain's olfactory center.

And Duft's mentolabial sulcus?

Don't get me started. Party's over.

Duft's scent has waned, and she is no longer amenable to mine. Our cellular humming dance, much like the Shimmy and the Jerk, is a thing of the past. Simply put, our endocrine and neurological systems no longer speak to one another. She has removed me from her buddy list.

Everything will never be the same.

Sucks to be me, dude.

And if that's not enough, Candelaria Chacon and Tetsuko Kendo make so much noise banging the life out of one another that many people grab their blankets and sleeping bags and move as far away from them as possible. Candy is a sport-fucking screamer, and she doesn't care who knows it. Every groaning, grunted squeal is a stab to the heart, a painful reminder of what it was like when Duft and I shared a bed, our tongues coiled like two pink snakes around one another, triggering the production of endorphins around the clock. We fell asleep one night like that, our tongues nestled inside the warm cave of each other's mouth. In the morning we danced together in the rain, her elflocks capturing that moment forever.

Now, when we get within two feet of one another, Duft's heroic defense system gains Herculean strength and valiantly takes a stand to protect her perfect little body...from me. She wrinkles up her nose, repelled by the trace residue of aluminum seeping from my pores, and motions for me to keep my distance. Her emotional restraining order prohibits anyone from getting close to her, and she likes that.

But my time in the tribal camp has not been fruitless. I have managed to purloin of one Duft's bras. Pressed inside each tiny cotton cup is a basil leaf. I carefully peel the soft, warm leaves from their b-cup molds and hold them to my face. The pungent aroma of sweet basil mingles with the perfume-oil of Duft's sweetly scented breasts. One leaf has a small indentation, probably where it nestled against Duft's peach-colored nipple. When I place that lucky leaf beneath my tongue, Duft's nectarous essence pops alive inside my mouth and I hear her little voice in the darkness where we once slept.

But Duft woke up. And now all she smells is the stench.

The plaque in my arteries harden.

It so sucks to be me.

Beth Redding makes an unannounced visit to various campsites, distributing leaflets with directions to the Pepper Ranch. Or at least that's the rumor. Nobody really saw her, but everyone seems to know somebody who was there when she passed by.

Kwame prays until he is delirious. He spends the entire night on his hands and knees, in the dirt, soiling himself, promising sacrifice after sacrifice if his request for imprecation is answered.

In his desperation, he calls on every saint he can think of to intercede on his behalf and negotiates complicated deals with each of them.

Just moments before the sun rises, Kwame passes out and falls face first into the dirt, his lucky penny clutched tightly in his fist.

Kwame will not hear the explosion that rocks the campground. He will be told about it later, and he will spend the rest of his days believing that he was somehow responsible.

For the others, the event will be seared into their memory cells for eternity, and they will go about their lives confused but guilt-free.

Dewey will forever link the explosion with his wet dream, while the Sittingdowns will boast that Junior's spastic colon was his frustrated attempt to warn them of danger.

Bob Bluitt will go to his grave believing that black helicopters circled the town only moments before, and that close-up infrared photographs were taken from somewhere in outer space, thus marking each and every one of them for future eradication.

Duft and Amy will tremble in each other's arms, supporting one another with warm hugs and soft, sisterly kisses.

Candelaria Chacon and Tetsuko Kendo will do what they do best—play with one another until they achieve simultaneous and bombastic orgasms. Then they will suck on each other's fingers and talk dirty, after which they will indulge in the practice of shrimping and tea-bagging.

Holsie Colldren and her husband will not go into panic mode. The old man will get on his corporate whore machine and see what the Net has to say, and Holsie will soothe her anxiety by eating the last of the pudding cups.

Dewey's boys don't even figure in the equation.

Oris Kumke will write in the police report that the only thing that saved him was "a case of the squirts," and that he owes his life to his loose bowels, which forced him to sleep behind a port-apotty, thus deflecting all the shrapnel.

Nobody will ever know what really happened. An explosion and fireball will shake the campsite, and when the blaze is extinguished and the smoke clears, Snake is nowhere to be found. Twelve hours later, after sifting through the blackened debris, enough Snake is found so that he can be buried. His coffin will be a borrowed Band-Aid box.

A confused Zinaida will spin and spin and spin, much like the local trout, going around and around in dizzying circles, asking the same simple question over and over again: "What happened? What happened?"

The same question will be asked by the police, the FBI, the media, and the surviving Wolfpack members.

When Kwame emerges from the smoking crater, his words rock the survivors: "There is a fungus among us."

The ensuing chaos and confusion will foster feelings of suspicion and distrust. Accusations, then threats, will fly about the camp, and verbal criticism will be replaced by physical assaults. Suspects will be called out by name, and the agitated accusers—mostly psychotically enraged Wolfpack club members—will call to account those who in any way might have wanted Snake out of the picture.

Walbert will be the first taken to task by the kangaroo court.

Bloodlust will replace the adrenalin flowing in everyone's veins and a posse will form almost immediately. Crush, aluminum bat in one hand and wire cutters in the other, will lead a group of enraged followers directly to Walbert. His interrogation will include ham-hock fist punches to the face and stomach, followed by a flurry of stomping kicks, and after insistently maintaining his innocence, they crank up the heat.

"Hang him by his testicle…if he's got one!"

Cooler heads prevail. Rather than sponsor a lynching, Crush elects instead to sever Walbert's testicles, and when Walbert is pantsed and pinned down, spread-eagle, on the dirt, Zinaida unexpectedly comes to his rescue. She says it would do no good to sever either of Walbert's testicles since they didn't work anyway.

Crush agrees, saying it would be a waste of time because, as he put it, "The little dude has whack jizz."

Zinaida concurs, confirming to the others once again that, "Walbert's spunk is bunk."

Crush decides instead to go with a more traditional punishment favored by Wolfpack alum in the past, and soon the word is spread that wire cutters will be used to amputate both of Walbert's big toes.

"And he'll do it," Zinaida warns. "He's speeding and he's not in any mood. Crush has served time, ya know."

Walbert begs for mercy, asks Crush if he will reconsider and take one of his testicles instead.

For Walbert, the gig is up, and he knows it. About to lose his testicles or his toes, all he can think about is losing Zinaida forever. His new mantra: No chance in hell.

Drained of all color, and obviously not his brutish self, Crush suddenly and unexpectedly cancels the torture session and calls a club meeting, buying Walbert at least a little time. Much like Dewey and his boys, Oris Kumke, and a few Wolfpack soldiers, Crush is racked with leg-buckling stomach cramps, followed by a burning torrent of diarrhea, leaving him weak and gasping for breath. Crush collapses before they can get back to the charred ruins of their biker camp.

Brahulyo Saucedo is summoned and immediately begins the healing process. Talking softly and rocking back and forth, eyes closed and head tilted towards his power source in the heavens, he gently rubs the distended bellies of the fish-eating five. Dewey refuses to let another man touch him in such an intimate manner and will remain incapacitated by the violent diarrhetic discharges long after the others have resumed eating solid food.

The explosion brings the party to an end and people begin finding ways out of town. Slowly traffic begins to unsnarl, and the numbers begin to diminish.

The funeral service is standard Wolfpack fare. Dewey's missing bottle of Jack Daniels mysteriously reappears and is passed among the club members, followed by lit joints and lines of meth, after which Snake's remains, packed into a Band-Aid box, are laid to rest in a six-by-six-by-six-inch hole in the campground soil. An impromptu eulogy is delivered, and Crush holds Zinaida close to him while she cries tears of confusion. Crush grinds up against Zinaida, encouraging her to let it all out.

Walbert watches from a safe distance, mindful of the foul-smelling posse's promise to separate him from his various body parts, but he needs to find out what Zinaida is going to do.

Stump Sittingdown has no time for the memorial service. He goes back to the spot where he left his car—running—and returns in a snit when he discovers it is nowhere to be found. Martha is hysterical; baby Sittingdown's diapers and extra pacifier were in the back seat. So was the Kroger's receipt, which served as his birth certificate.

But they run into three teenagers, desperate for cash, who promise to take them where they want to go in exchange for gas money.

"Decision time, Daddy," Martha tells Stump. She jiggles Junior in her arms. "Time for Daddy to make up his mind."

"I hear there's a whole valley near here filled with mutant sheep. There was a mass impregnation done. Supposed to be around here somewhere. Anyone know where?" Stump tries to read their faces. He won't allow his family in a car with just anybody.

"We could take you to see the white buffalo. We know where that is," the teenage driver says, hopeful for a gas-paying passenger or two.

Stump is unsure. "Well, we really wanted to see the sheep."

"We can find out on the way," the driver suggests. "Just get in."

"We eventually want to get to Pepper Ranch," Stump tells them. "You're going there, right?"

The driver is not so sure. He checks with his friends. They confer briefly, then decide they have to be back home for school on Monday. "We're not really ready to leave the planet yet or anything, but we can take you as far as Happy Valley."

Stump hasn't heard about that and he is intrigued.

Dewey strolls through the smoking ash and dust, munching on an ice cream cone. What a fool. Doesn't he know?

"This good," he says, licking the deadly wafer.

Enjoy your deathsicle, ya fucking moron.

Transportation is sorted out. Cars are found, cars are lost, and rides are negotiated.

When the Wolfpack roars through camp on their way to Pepper Ranch, Zinaida is firmly planted behind Crush, her arms wrapped tightly around his newly distended belly. Crush is still pale and sweating profusely, but when he passes Walbert, he tells him, "She's mine now."

Walbert flops in the dirt and cries like a baby.

Briola takes a long drink of her precious ambrosia and kicks at Walbert. "We gotta get going."

"In a minute," Walbert blubbers.

"No, now," Briola says, and nudges her sobbing husband once again.

"How about a little love," Walter wails. "I'm about to lose a nut here."

"What's it matter," Briola says.

Eco-terrorists are offering rides to anyone willing to help spike old-growth timber and weaken the stress joints of ski lifts, and although Dewey and his boys find the vandalism to be "wholesome and for reals," they decline, setting their sights instead on the Pepper Ranch, much like everyone else.

The party atmosphere returns and everyone is anxious to get back on the road and move as a complete, albeit dysfunctional, unit to the next event; each a parasite unto him or herself, attaching to whatever available host is capable of supplying the nourishing stew necessary to fill the gaping hole of sadness and futility in each of their souls.

Confused and angry (and dangerously low on narcotics), the Wolfpack leaves town. Snake's death—and ersatz funeral—has already become nothing more than a memory-hit, something to talk about later down the road.

The bikers leave, the dust clears, and most of the fires get extinguished.

Everything changes the same.

Within the once-somber sea of sadness, sudden and unexpected bursts of touch-alerts. Everywhere. With the brain chemistry now involved, the mechanism of pain is olfacted, then broken down.

They're all doing it—touching, connecting, uniting into one fulfilled wholeness.

Nasal appraisal.

Duft's fingers lightly brush Amy's hair as she walks past her, and a bombardment of libidinal thought missiles are exchanged. They giggle and poke their tongues at one another, storing for future use in the limbic lobe portion of their energized brains, memories of that instant's joy and pleasure that they will be able to recall at a capricious moment's notice.

In order to accomplish this, however, my emotional memories have to be evicted. Duft's hypothalamus now sends messages to the new tenant in her pituitary: Amy. Different hormones are produced and released that will attach themselves to no other receptor sites other than those belonging to Amy, and once Duft's odor molecules target those sites, her sensory system stimulates her into a born-again state of sexual arousal. Duft's downy soft body hairs, once lazy and lethargic, now stiffen at the sight—and scent—of Amy.

Their pheromones allow them to sense the presence of one another, even in total darkness, and this they do with frequency and ease. Amy's odor molecules are allowed entrance into the once-fiercely guarded Duft compound, where they trigger a seemingly endless firing of neuron nerve cells. Duft's bipolar receptor cell is back in action and, more importantly, Duft is humming once again. Her plump little love button pulsates at a thumping 95 beats per minute.

Step aside. Make a place for another.

Oops, already did. Never mind.

Candy Chacon and Tetsuko Kendo cruise by in the air-conditioned luxury of a brand-new silver Lexus.

Dewey, playing a game of pocket pool, gawks as they roll past.

Candy Chacon slides the tinted electric window down. "Now play this tape: I am so done with you." She sticks her pink, pierced tongue out at him.

Dewey continues playing with himself.

"We have A/C. And wanna know something else?" Candy laughs, then slithers down the seat, out of sight. Tetsuko gives a start as Candelaria works her magic on him.

"Hey," Tetsuko yells out at Dewey. "I'm just trying to keep her alive and happy."

Laughing, they roll out of Straystar.

A couple of the boys attempt to commiserate with Dewey.

"The old burp 'n slurp. That's messed up, dude."

"All shady and shit, huh?"

"Dude. Bobbin' and slobbin' like that? That is so janked up. I crap you negative."

Bob Bluitt is next to roll. Dangerously low on gas, he cannot afford the luxury of stopping to say goodbye. He toots the horn of his battered Honda as he drives past, and shouts out the word, "Molecular."

"Who was that?" someone asks.

Kwame tries to restore order amid the chaos, but it's hopeless. Fearful that Oris Kumke will find him, Kwame decides to bolt. He will look for the others after he's hit the open highway.

But Oris Kumke has attached himself to Holsie Colldren and her husband as a kind of Zinaida clone, nuking snacks and tending to Holsie's husband's needs. Truth is, he can't even remember Kwame's name.

When I approach Duft—who, along with Amy, is trying to organize a last-minute recycling effort with all the garbage—she holds a hand up, warning me to stay back. I'm not sure, but I think she pinches her nostrils closed. She tells me not to worry about a ride, that she and Amy will be fine. Amy puts a tiny arm around Duft's perfect waist and leads her away, their hips swaying in metronomic unison. I think I hear Amy say, "He kind of doesn't get it."

As for the others…who gives a shit.

Nothing is like it was. Things will be the same no more forever.

I'm out of here.

I later hear that Straystar was evacuated almost overnight once the traffic start moving, leaving behind hundreds of smoldering and still-burning campfires that, fueled by seasonal Chinook winds, re-ignited and consumed some 400,000 acres of forest before the raging fire burned itself out, literally obliterating Straystar (and three other towns) from the face of the Earth. (Everyone just assumes that the cure turd was somehow miraculously spared, although, to the best of my knowledge, nobody has ever actually seen her.)

I remember little of the mountain drive, the directional signs flashing by in a blur every few miles, the fender benders, stalled vehicles and hitchhikers.

Soot, smoke and ash.

I wore Duft's bra around my neck like a cotton necklace, the scent of her dissipating with the passing of each mile marker posted alongside the road. I ate the basil leaf one sunrise and cried for the next 400 miles.

But memory is the essence of what shapes our perception of reality and, like masturbation, if you're not into it, it's too much like work. So, time to move on. The processed-food industry is my church now. Or is it my religion? Doesn't matter. I am the new TV. And the new season is about to begin.

Time to rewrite reality. Stay tuned.

*****

The post-coital daze following the Cure Girl lovefest has all but disappeared. Newfound devotees are nonetheless sucked in daily, thanks to the demagoguery of AM talk radio hosts and media coverage ad nauseam. The nationwide network of interstates hosts the greatest number of vehicles it has ever experienced. Word is out. The floodgates have been opened. All roads lead to Pepper Ranch.

The nation's arteries, so much like my own, are hopelessly clogged.

One look will tell you everything you need to know about these people—they are starving. And I am hating them for their hunger.

Parasites adapting to a new host body. *Feed me!*

Throw the monkeys a cookie and watch them dance.

Time to think clearly now.

I've listened to enough of Duft's rants to know that when the brain produces dopamine and norepinephrine, distinct changes in mood and behavior take place; the ability to think more quickly, react more rapidly to stimuli, and feel more attentive, motivated, and mentally energetic.

Pure surges of brain power.

The chemical mood modifiers are already present in the brain. All I need to do is tap into the catecholamines.

In order to get there, I need to synthesize the alertness chemicals, and I do this with amino acids. Fueled by their energy, I can retreat to my clandestine neurotransmitter lab where I manufacture tyrosine, punching into the brain a command to create more and more of the alertness chemicals.

Flying.

Doesn't take much to rise above the others, most of whom suffer from the same general malaise—fatigue, a dull achiness, and headaches.

Why do I do it? It's just so easy.

And the birds. Birds have been falling and dropping from the sky with a new and urgent frequency, probably dead before they hit the ground. Everyone seems to think it's the result of the choking acrid smoke and ash from the raging inferno left behind in Straystar.

Dewey suffers a broken nose and lacerated forehead when a two-pound crow plummets from the sky and slams itself into his face while he is scorching up a side road at 85 miles an hour.

Dead birds everywhere. Mostly blue jays and crows, but once in a while a robin plops to the pavement without warning.

Walbert's all but gone over the edge. After his toes and testicles were spared, his immediate thought was to get out of Dodge, but Briola is adamant that they stay and see it through. Back in Spanish Pork, Utah, they pledged to one another to stick it out until they either found the Fountain of Youth (which did not exist), the Doomsday Asteroid (which they weren't allowed to see), or whatever awaits them now at Pepper Ranch, and Briola demands that he keep his word to her.

Walbert fears that if he remains with the group they will castrate or kill him. He wants the suspicion and blame for Snake's demise to be passed along to somebody else—maybe Amy or Dewey—but somehow he will have to convince the others of their obvious guilt. Walbert has managed to stay close behind Holsie Colldren's R.V. since departing Straystar, but has lost sight of everyone else in the smoky fog. He still feels connected to the group and will remain with Holsie and her husband (and Oris Kumke) until he can figure out what to do next.

But it's no thing. None of it matters.

Smoky mirrors.

Out of the mountains and into an overcrowded campground. The size of our group has diminished, but the intensity remains unchanged. New hope of a fresh beginning provides sustenance for the starving, and like eager schoolchildren on a field trip, they chatter and laugh endlessly when they see one another again.

I don't bother counting heads. I know who's here and who is not. And it really doesn't matter. Most of the people in the group have been following me. It's not just their moral compass that is broken. Where I go, they go.

Brahulyo Saucedo tells us that something inside each one of us needs correction, and we all know that. Repent to God and bury the bone, he says. And we all know that too.

Open yourself to correction and make it righteous.

Yes, yes and yes.

If you want it, say Amen.

Amen!

But we have other issues right now.

Because of the new forest fires—some of which are still burning out of control with a paltry 2 percent containment—campfires and grills are outlawed. All cooking now has to be done in Holsie's R.V. and this does not please Holsie's old man, or Oris

Kumke, for that matter. Most people just come in long enough to make a plate and leave.

Everyone is expected to contribute something on an honor system but rarely does the tip jar contain enough to cover the cost of expenses, and Holsie's old man lets everyone know it. While he sits locked in at the remodeled dinette, which now serves as his "lab," where he can manipulate his corporate whore machine (or become manipulated, he's no longer sure which is which), he harangues and bullies the feedees for cash.

"Or at least some groceries. Jesus, is that gonna kill ya?"

But there is no place to buy groceries from. It's a two-hour park on the on-ramp before squeezing onto the interstate, and from there it's touch and go, bumper to bumper, a crawl, a standstill. The move is in slow motion. All exit ramps and merging lanes blocked, unmoving.

Dewey and the boys had been nose-to-ass to an SUV for the past thirty hours and had not traveled eight miles. At one point, traffic had stopped for so long that they shut the engine off and ran across several fields to a convenience store, where all that remained on the shelves were gumballs and Life Savers. (They took what they could and left without paying.)

Crush had been exhibiting flu-like symptoms only hours before they were able to identify his corpse. He had abandoned Zinaida near an exit ramp, annoyed with her incessant whining about the huge number of mosquito bites she had suffered since they began riding on his motorcycle, and took the Pack with him. They could make good time on the interstate, driving through, between, and around, four-wheeled vehicles. The best guess is that Crush died on his bike, managed to maintain stability for some unspecified amount of time before listing to the left and then ramming, face first, into an oncoming tanker trunk. (Miraculous how it all works out—we die on the last day of our lives.)

Zinaida will not be told about the accident and will never know what became of Crush.

Holsie took pity on the splotchy, scabby, bloodied Zinaida, her hair whipped unrecognizable by the force of the open wind, as she stood by the side of the road, crying. She spotted Zinaida a half mile ahead of them, but Zinaida would not (or could not) respond to her hand waves.

It was two hours before they could reach Zinaida, and when they did, she simply stepped into the R.V. when Holsie opened the door.

Zinaida had been eaten alive by mosquitoes and ticks, no doubt about that. But her neck, breasts, and stomach, were covered with mighty hickeys, a kind of going away present from Crush.

"What are you watching?" Zinaida wants to know. "And what's *he* doing here?"

"I've got better than 20/20 vision," Oris Kumke tells Zinaida, "so I know exactly who you are. I'm in charge here, helping run the website. So just stay out of things."

"Who cares," Zinaida says. "I just want to lay down and drink hot soup."

"I don't know how you're gonna do that," Oris says. "Every damn body is gonna run out of gas at the same time. Then what? Where's your soup then? Ignoranus."

"I need a comb and some lotion," Zinaida says loudly. She scratches at her bleeding arms and face. "Put something on me. It's like ants under my skin."

Holsie reluctantly decides to trust Oris Kumke behind the wheel. They are barely traveling inches at a time, and there is no passing. Everyone is locked in. It seems safe enough, and Oris Kumke insists he is up to the task.

Three hours later they are out of gas and parked in the HOV lane, playing pinochle.

Amy and Duft put their heads together and come up with a

medicinal paste made from herbs and weeds picked from the ditch running alongside the interstate, which they smear liberally on the ballooning, puffed-up flesh of Zinaida. It seems to have a soothing and calming effect on her, although in her feverish state she insists she can hear music that no one else can. She says that everyone should repent to God and bury the bone.

Me, I can't take my eyes off Duft. When she throws her head back and laughs at something Amy says, I fixate upon the downy silkiness of her vibrissae.

Excitotoxicity.

My stares provoke the Stink Eye from Duft and Amy. They know what's inside my head.

No secret. You can't smell it in the air, but trust me. It's over. Duft can never unbecome who she is; I cannot become who I am not. This one's in the books.

Love is a lucky place. Where I'm at sucks shit.

But enough about me.

Zinaida's condition worsens. Someone finally says it: *West Nile Virus.* It's all over the news. How could you *not* know about it. Somebody else suggests it was Rocky Mountain spotted fever. Another disease, another disaster—add that to the palette of our ultimate and imminent destruction and you got a recipe for real disaster. Whatever it is, we're in a viral foot race and falling way behind.

Nobody knows what to do, and many think it's too late anyway. For everyone. It's already upon us, but still they pray for guidance from Beth, the little monkey Messiah that started all of this.

And then—*snap!*—just like that. Like every other miracle, mine comes to me in a mind-numbing rush when it's least expected.

The Voice is back.

Invisible things suddenly made clear.

Teamwork will make the dream work. After all, we are the future generation of princes and priests, destined, each one of us, for breathtaking success. Beth—or anyone of her ilk—will be no match for our numbers. Not now.

And my divine assignment in all of this? First things first.

We need a new, sanctified strength for the journey ahead of us. Every digitally encoded bit of genome stuffed inside each one of us—justified or condemned—will rise to the occasion. You'll see.

You will all see.

Someone—somewhere, somehow—has disrespected each of us in a mighty way. Up to me now to show the way.

Call me Butter, 'cause I'm on a roll.

The plan's a simple one, cooked up in the persistent chaos of my own head while I sleep and walk through life.

Let me break it down for you:

Heat, fires, drought, brown clouds, space junk, global warming, Chronic Wasting Disease, West Nile Virus, AIDS, international terrorism, Dewey's breath, every environmental insult imaginable set upon us, and then some. If the cure turd is right, and the end is near, then it could all be gone at any moment.

But is she prophet, or just the whore of Babylon?

Savior…or anti-Christ?

Nostradamus says we have until 3797 before things totally collapse. Atlantis is supposed to rise in 2014. The Maya predict it's all over in 2012 (December 22, to be precise). Beth tells us we have a matter of weeks, maybe months (hard to pin her down).

The Reckoning? Guess we'll have to see.

The Rapture? I'll call you.

I do know this: Once this little situation is over, we will rejoice and live in peace. Guaran-damn-teed.

Holsie's old man has provided me with all the ammunition I need to fight the cure turd. His days aren't spent just downloading porn off the Net (although it does consume an enormous amount of his free time). I put him on the payroll weeks ago and he has supplied me with enough data so that I can now counter her prediction of an imminent apocalypse with facts.

Beth's vision of world events and natural disasters are really just a manifestation of her own paranoid imagination and fear. Her belief that the droughts and wildfires are a harbinger of world's end is nothing more than random weather patterns occurring all over the planet.

Don't believe me?

Try tuning in to the Weather Channel once in a while. El Niño, La Niña, Los Piñata—no matter. It doesn't take a genius to figure out that even a dead monkey will float downstream. Hell, even Gravy Brains knows that.

The Book of Revelations—which Beth borrows so liberally from to support her prophecies—was in reality a last-minute addition to the Bible, referencing events that were taking place at the time it was written, and never intended as a literal prediction of a future thousands of years hence.

According to Holsie's old man (or at least the information he is feeding me), apocalypse actually means "revelation."

In your face, Beth!

And the word "pagan" comes from the Latin *Paganis*, meaning "people of the countryside."

Do the math, people.

Beth, with all her freewheeling jibba-jab, is doing nothing more than providing an excuse for not looking at the long-term consequences of our own actions.

Beth is forcing her prophecy to occur. And we are letting her get away with it.

Face it, civilization is—and has always been—on the decline, and, as citizens of this Earth, we have abdicated our spiritual responsibilities. Price to be paid.

But, according to my sources, the Book of Revelations is all about Rome anyway. And isn't there something in there about Rome being the whore of Babylon? (Sounds like someone I know.)

Mama mia!

Apocalypse, annihilation, the Second Coming, the Rapture, the Reckoning—call it what you will. Candy's dandy, but before the Lord can return, the anti-Christ must be manifested. This monster will present himself as divine and work all kinds of bogus miracles with the devil's aid and deceive many.

Hello!

Then—and only then—Christ will return and destroy him (or her?).

Beth is just the opening act, but she's got no finishing move. Truth is, no one is coming to save us. We are rushing headlong towards our own end, with the cure turd leading us all to slaughter, shaking like a bunch of red-assed baboons riding the mercy seat all the way to Pecker Ranch.

I need something—a sign, so that the others can see—just to let Beth know I am not fucking around here.

The Voice *and* the Vision. The ultimate endorsement.

A Third Eye!

You heard me. Not just any third eye, but something permanent—a brand!—for all to see (and be seen by!)—sealed on my forehead. And if that's not enough, hold onto your hats, *self-trepanation*. A gaping maw bored right through that third eye into the very brain itself, where every bit of information—verbal, aural, or written—can be recorded, sorted, classified and (if necessary) debunked.

The truth will set us all free!

Can I get an Amen?

Rise, puppets!

Motivation and momentum is what moves a vision to

completion. Lose momentum and you lose your place at the head of the pack. You are doomed to follow. And I will not allow that to happen.

That's why this third eye will be much more than a mere symbol. It will be the catalyst I will use to understand her (know thine enemy!), or, better yet, confuse her. It is a humble man's shock-and-awe approach before the ultimate onslaught (read head-drilling) to discover who/what she really is. There can be no victory without a fight, and make no mistake about it—we are at war. The hole in my head will do more than bring light into a dark world, it will reveal the path to righteousness, and the giant-killer will emerge.

Killer of infidels.

Slay the giants that rise up against us.

It won't be done *by* me; it will be done *through* me.

Hey, if you're in for a penny, you're in for a pound.

You crap-rats can float your p.c. b.s. all you want, but here on planet Earth... .

Ehh, who cares.

Get saved! Don't be wayward in your salvation. You will never accomplish your divine destiny without the anointing.

While Duft and Amy dishonor their bodies with vile affections, I think of ways to turn hydrogen into a never-ending energy source. Why don't they work on that? Yeah. Uh-huh. Everyone gets a smile on that one.

When I bring up my plans for self-trepanation at dinner, Dewey is most impressed.

"You'll be in the *Guinness Book Of*, dude!"

Holsie's old man wants to digitally film the event and sell it live over the Internet, amassing what he envisions to be a small fortune for just a couple of hours' work. "Suicides are one thing, but this is something else."

Duft and Amy pretend not to even hear. Instead, they loudly

voice their anger and disgust against violent, mindless zealots who kill and subjugate in His name.

"Would Jesus kill an abortion doctor with a high-powered rifle while he was eating his breakfast?"

"Prolly not," Amy finishes Duft's thought. They smile beatifically at one another, then bump their tiny fists triumphantly.

Dewey is awed by the idea, and salivates. "Total functification."

He hops about in the cramped R.V. "Dude, we could all drill holes in our heads. Be like a big tribe or some shit. The Holey Heads!"

"We could maybe communicate without even talking," guesses one of his boys. "Just *think* shit."

"Oh, dude."

The reverie is broken when a roving pack of infuriated strangers try to force their way into the already crowded R.V., looking for handouts, or something to drink. When Holsie's old man refuses even more mouths to feed, mob mentality consumes the outsiders and they angrily rock the R.V. from side to side, almost tipping it over. Despite Duft's and Amy's plaintive appeals for self-control, angry epithets are hurled back and forth. The situation quickly gets out of control.

Holsie Colldren splashes hot bean soup on some of the mob, burning her hands in the process.

"Go 'way!" she shrieks.

"We're just asking you to share," a woman cries. "I have a baby out here."

Holsie's old man wheels to a window, peers out. No baby in sight.

"Lyin' bitch," he fumes. "Put some more soup on!"

Knocked from stem to stern, pillar to post, Duft manages to right herself and get to the damaged fiberglass door.

"Here," she shouts, and throws out several bubble packs of vitamins and supplements. They are quickly ground to dust beneath the boots of the angry mob. They will not be bought off with trinkets. These people want *at least* a pound of flesh.

Teeth chattering and ears abuzz, Zinaida points a trembling hand at the faux leather kitchenette booth, where the Sittingdowns are sitting down.

"What? What are you lookin' at us for?" Stump is uncomfortable and stuffs Junior protectively into the warm nest-cave between himself and Martha. "Quit it."

Zinaida is sweating profusely. "Under," she gasps.

"Under what," Stump snarls.

The R.V. rocks wildly, stressing out the axles and cross members. Everyone is showered with plasticware, boxes of cereal, and prepackaged foodstuffs.

"Seat," Zinaida blubbers.

"Quit lookin' at us!" Stump is red-faced, becoming angrier at the moment. Zinaida is giving them the Stink Eye and he does not like it one bit.

Kwame is flushed with a sudden burst of adrenalin. Take charge time.

"Everybody up!"

As difficult as it is, everyone manages to slide out of the booth, bodies pressed against one another before getting knocked to the floor. Dewey grins lecherously as he flops on top of Amy, who is pinned helplessly, face down, onto the floor, trying to crawl to Duft. He tries to hump her without seeming too obvious, then throws propriety to the four winds and rides her tiny frame like a bucking bronco.

Kwame tries to read Zinaida. He flips the lid of the seat up and stares in amazement at the Tommy gun stashed ages ago by Snake and his Wolfpack brethren.

"Out of the way, people!" Kwame pulls the weapon from its

hiding place and staggers to the gaping hole where the door once was.

"Be gone!" Kwame brandishes the Tommy gun, but the sight of him armed with a weapon frightens and angers them even more, and they retaliate by rocking the vehicle with an even fiercer intensity.

Barely able to keep his balance, Kwame somehow manages to release the safety on the vintage machine gun and, without further warning, fires a short burst out the door and through the flimsy walls of the R.V., dispersing the mob.

Shell casings tinkle to the floor…then silence.

"Wow," is all Kwame can say. He hefts the Tommy gun in his hands, the weight of it empowering him.

"You can get off now," Amy bristles.

"Just trying to protect you from friendly fire," Dewey grunts, breathless.

Bob Bluitt gets to his feet. Nobody even knew he was in the R.V. "They had animal eyes," he says.

"You okay?" Amy asks.

"I think so," Dewey says, rolling and grinding across Amy's buttocks. The hideous grin on his face indicates the lewd pleasure he is robbing from Amy.

"I'm not talking to you, butt-hole! Duft?"

"Yes," Duft says, squirming to sit up. "Are you?"

"I will be when numb nuts gets off!"

Dewey laughs a nervous laugh, says to no one in particular that now he wants a cigarette.

Oris Kumke extricates himself from the tangle of arms and legs, and whistles at Kwame.

"I held back from capping their dumb asses 'cause I didn't want to hit anybody in here, then you let loose with a fucking machine gun. Didn't think you had it in you, Rambo."

Kwame hefts the Tommy gun in his hands. It feels good.

"The shit storm is upon us."

"Welcome to the Hate State," Oris Kumke says.

Everyone gets to their feet. A hasty group examination reveals nothing more serious than scrapes and bruises. The contents of the R.V. are damaged, and the undercarriage is probably damaged beyond repair. Not that we were going anywhere anyway.

"What do we do now?" Martha Sittingdown asks, surreptitiously sipping from one of her water jugs.

"Somebody could help me pick up," Holsie says.

Gradually, everyone begins to shuffle around inside the cramped quarters.

"So, are you still gonna do it, dude?" Dewey licks his lips in anticipation.

Yes, I'm still gonna do it.

Dewey wonders where we'll get a drill.

First things first.

The mark.

Oris Kumke surrenders his Brooklyn Bullwhip. With Holsie's old man's needle-nose pliers, I fashion a branding iron. Several minutes over the propane-fueled range in Holsie's R.V. heats the cheap metal into a white-hot surgical weapon.

Everyone is hushed, silent. They can only stare.

Once you get a taste of the visceral underbelly of the Great Beast, you are never the same. Trust me. It hardens in the brain like a big black tumor and it just keeps growing in that dark, untouched place.

Several deep breaths to steady the hand and ease the palpitations, then—no turning back now—I take aim and sear the scarring shape of the Third Eye into my own flesh. Right between the eyes. Blueprint to the soul.

Skin is the body's largest organ, covering some twenty square feet and weighing almost six pounds. Hundreds of small nerves send impulses to the brain, interpreting physical pressure, pain, and other assorted sensations. But I can't tell if everything's working right or not. I do not feel a thing.

The hot metal burns through the first keratin layer instantly, cooking the epidermis, searing its way past the dermis, and scorching with ease the subcutaneous tissue into a sizzling and blistered ooze, charring my skin and blood into a festering and permanent scar, stinking the room up with my own barbecued meat.

I have shown them *how*. They will have to *do*.

Everyone screams, scramble all over one another. The stench is overpowering.

I sneak a peek at Duft. The final image I have of her: Her tiny erector pili muscles do what they're programmed to do and goose bumps erupt all over her body. Her eyes widen, her pupils dilate. She faints.

This pleases me.

Why she is so disturbed by the scent is beyond me. You'd think she would be used to contextually discordant odors. After all, a woman's armpits are much smellier than a man's. Surely she's come to terms with the salts, water, and milky substances under Amy's arms and around her nipples, secreted by her apocrine glands. Her bacteria digests those milky substances and create byproducts that makes her sweat so stinky, but, like peas in a pod and birds of a feather, Duft doesn't seem to have a problem with the gaminess of Amy.

But I digress.

Even Dewey had to admit, "Like a train wreck, dude. I had to look." He hands me a small mirror. He really is salivating.

Difficult to see through the red curtain, but the third eye doesn't look like a third eye. Not to me. It more closely resembles an egg. Or a bull's eye. Hard to tell. Each heartbeat jettisons a pulsating stream of something red and orange out at whatever is in front of me. And my eyes are swelling shut. Big fat pancakes.

Doesn't matter.

The average human has twelve pints of blood circulating throughout their body. I donate at least three of those to the cause.

May we hear the inspired word of a supreme and loving God.

"Zinaida just had some kind of seizure," Amy says, crying, cradling an unconscious Duft in her small arms.

I smell what I hear. I hear what I taste. I taste what I see. Inhabited, I must ride it out.

Total functification.

Inhale. Exhale.

Sky slaughter.

The tattoo-brand will have to do for now. Until the actual skull-piercing, the mark will serve as a beacon of light to the others who are so quickly losing their way. Those who can, will follow.

The rest? Plenty of room at the end of the line, sugar feet.

Somebody vomits. A turbulence of agonizing perfume. I suddenly become sleepy.

Breakfast is waking up in a zoo cage.

Dewey's foul breath. "He is too gonna make it!"

Who does it suck more than to be me.

Bob Bluitt, pumped up with a newfound enthusiasm, begins assembling his army from a never-ending stream of dazed and vulnerable stragglers. He knows the helicopters will be back soon, only this time they'll be doing more than just taking pictures. In possession now of every encoded bit of each person's signature DNA information, laser-guided smart bombs will hunt us down, one by one. He notes too that roving gangs, armed with handguns and brickbats, are forming alliances with militant groups and rounding up civilians, stripping them of their clothing, jewelry, cash and identification.

People are robbed at gunpoint, beaten senseless, and left for dead. Everyone wants to get to New Land. The realized fear is that we are already there.

Time to get out of Dodge.

Holsie's old man uses what little time is left to download as much material from his laptop as he can onto diskettes before all power is lost. Glued to the corporate whore machine, he is fascinated by one of the new Net programs/reality shows—suicides captured like via web cam (his inspiration for charging big bucks for the self-trepanation).

The corporate whore machine has now become the "world wide waste" of Holsie's old man's time. A fickle mistress indeed. Every time he attempts to download the moving images of someone ending their life, the system crashes. Undeterred, he reboots and starts from scratch.

Dewey watches him through a window while he pisses on the R.V. Holsie's man cautions whoever is within earshot: "Government can see everything we do, through our monitors. Their software makes them work like cameras. *Always* unplug your monitor when you do anything freaky or illegal."

Dewey just laughs at him. "Talk about the government. What about you? Gettin' a little too exuberated, aren't you, perv?"

Dewey accuses him of wanting to bump uglies with the corpses.

"Get off yer pedastool, dude," Dewey snarls. "Think we can't see what's happening from out here? You're gettin' a big ol' Colorado chubby. Don't tell me, we can see it from here."

Walbert is sullen and morose. Before her unexpected demise, Zinaida kept going on about how there were two kinds of Catholic girls—the ones who put out, and those who go through life with their knees bolted together. She wanted everyone to know that in spite of her recent indiscretions with Snake *and* Crush, she was a member in good standing of the latter group. Believe it or not.

Walbert is uncomfortable with the pattern of loss he is beginning to see in his life—Briola's affection, various body parts, and now Zinaida. He alone feels responsible for all that has gone wrong. Briola tells him to let it go; that once they get to

Pepper Ranch, everyone will be made whole and they will both be able to communicate with Zinaida again.

A few words are said over Zinaida's bloated corpse, and she is laid to rest inside the R.V., wrapped in a sleeping bag. There just isn't any time to give her a proper burial.

Can't stay. Have to walk from here. Everyone is instructed to take with them whatever they can carry.

Like suspects in a lineup, everybody queues up outside the bullet-riddled R.V. Holsie Colldren opens up her last camera for one final group photo.

Stalled and burning vehicles have produced such a choking toxic haze that it has completely obliterated the poison-gas cloud that has hung over this valley for the past fifty years. The Brown Cloud, the pride of the mountain west for half a century, is no more. Well, it's still there…it just can't be seen.

Apparently Holsie and her old man have come to an understanding. He will stay behind, awaiting U.S. troops who will surely come to his aid, and when he is in the safe arms of his liberators, he will call her and make arrangements for their reunion. His food cache consists mostly of Doritos and pizza rolls. Dewey sells him two cans of beer.

Time, or lack thereof, is the thing. Thousands of people have already started the trek westward, towards the mountains. A surprising number of them take their pets with them, although small herds of confused dogs and cats run free.

Amy and Duft ooh and ah when Dewey snags a frantic greyhound and fashions a makeshift leash out of his belt.

"You're gonna thank me for this later," he says.

Amy and Duft lose their smiles. They look into each other's eyes, droopy and sad.

Me, I walk the light now, though you'd never know it. I hardly know it myself.

A makeshift headband packed with shaved ice. Good as new.

From what I hear, Kwame still clutches the Tommy gun. No one seems to notice, or care.

Anxious for the order to move out, I inhale the self-consciousness of all the little campers clutching their meager possessions, awaiting the purity of safe comfort promised so long ago.

And then it's go time. We are heading home.

Surprisingly, Holsie doesn't seem all that concerned about leaving her husband behind. "We'll come back for you," she tells him, with a flippant wave of the hand, though she doesn't really explain how that will happen.

"Yeah, but when?" His question falls on deaf ears. "I'll call you," he promises.

Over the foothills, then up into the mountains.

Duft and Amy, consoling each other with soft cooing sounds, power-walk side by side in total body synchrony, their backpacks bumping against their fannies. They never let go of one another's hand, and for that reason they stumble a lot.

Behind us, the constant *pop! pop! pop!* of small-arms fire, followed by hysterical screams. Nihilistic gangs of thugs make quick work of the weak and unprotected, which pretty much describes Holsie's old man. He never stood a chance.

The acrid stench of the deadly air dissolves into an obscene mephitis created from tons of fecal matter and urine, creating a deadly cocktail served up for all to imbibe.

No one looks behind. They can't afford to. We need to face what's ahead of us:

Fences—trampled, cut or destroyed. Cattle, sheep and horses—ranged free with antelope, deer, elk and bison—bring a superficial natural order back to everything, except the domesticated animals, much like Holsie's old man, are ill-equipped for freedom and don't stand a ghost of a chance. Bigger bull's-eyes on their backs than Holsie's old man had.

Stupid things walking around in a dull daze. No match for the heavy one-two punch of total anarchy.

Anything in the way gets broken, slaughtered or eaten.

Corpses, always found nude, dot the foothills. Clothes are at a premium.

The hottest, driest summer in history, but heat cannot stop the multitudes who are scrambling for their very lives.

The scenic vista as we trek across the hills:

Barricaded shop windows, greed mongers, madmen and political conspirators, terrorists, road rage, perversion, corpses, blown-up buildings. Real live animal attacks.

Unheroic times. The zeitgeist of America in the 21st Century.

Destined for sanctification, we move on, traveling into a far country, covering the land like a cloud, heading for the big dance with bug-eyed hopes that there will be someone to dance with once we get there.

Step aside. Make a place for another.

News choppers cram-jam available airspace. Bob Bluitt zigs and zags, evading the many spotlights from above that comb the foothills and mountains.

A field reporter from a Denver-based action news team becomes furious with his photographer because his hair doesn't look right, and he punches the poor slob out. Now he's got messy hair *and* a blank screen. Doesn't matter much. He is jumped, beaten into insensibility, and robbed of all his clothes. If that's not enough, vulgar profanities are scrawled all over his nude body. The camera is repositioned, and live videotape of his pale, flabby torso is video-streamed via satellite back to his unsuspecting co-anchors, who stare in horror at their news team member's desecrated anatomy.

"Okay, I'm not sure what we're looking at here," Kim, at the action news desk, says vapidly. Perplexed, she looks to her co-anchor, the prettier of the two.

Lisa, the cute little Mexican news reader, squints at her monitor. "It looks like—my god, is it? Should we be looking at this?"

"Maybe we should go to commercial," Kim suggests.

Pretty Lisa trembles, repulsed by the reality of what they are feeding the public. She turns to Kim, who has lost all ability to speak.

A newsroom intern screams in the background. The image disappears from everyone's television screen.

Campfires blaze, get out of hand, then burn completely out of control, turning night into day. Shirtless men in war paint stomp through the hot cinders, setting off more fires.

Ant-people scurry and scatter like confused cockroaches with nowhere to go.

Onward, soldiers.

Nobody wants to stop and camp for the night, fearful of marauding bands of cutthroats.

Rumor mill has it that special-ops troops will parachute into the gathering mass to try and gain some control, and perhaps bring food and water.

It does not happen.

Pilotless drones buzz the mountains and hilltops, sending Bob Bluitt into further fits of delusional paranoia. Fearful of becoming a recognizable target of opportunity, he alters his appearance and changes clothes constantly, but he steadfastly keeps his dream alive. He remains convinced he will soon have his own army of big-breasted blonde bimbos with shaved pudenda who will do whatever he says. It is all that keeps him going.

The bulk of the mob skirts a major fire by circling northwards, still moving west.

We counter by peeling off into the opposite direction, seeking shelter in an arroyo near an abandoned mine. Kwame heroically guards our flank.

Though our numbers are sorely diminished, the core group remains constant: Kwame, the Sittingdowns, Walbert and Briola, Duft and Amy, Holsie Colldren, Dewey and one of his boys (whom he has now taken to calling his lieutenant).

A campfire is built and everyone hunkers around it for warmth.

Odor might be the quickest way to trigger nostalgic reverie, but the rancid b.o. and unwashed hair in this ragtag army gives birth to just one more environmental disaster to deal with.

Amy and Duft find a small pool where they can clean one another with biodegradable soap (and I love them for that). The others seem content to reek. The smell of fear is everywhere.

Everyone's too frightened and nervous to eat, although Dewey comes up with some concoction he calls *arroz con peros*. When Kwame derisively suggests to the others that they should avoid the "mystery meat," Dewey calls him a butt-munch and threatens to withhold his portion of tomorrow's breakfast—puppy stew.

Dewey snaps his heels together, places two fingers beneath his nostrils.

"Hey, Adolf Shitler, I cooked it just the way you like it—El Dante."

"Then eat, if you want to end up with food poisoning," Kwame snarls, "again! You're condemned to repeat the past."

"Go back to Russia, pole smoker," Dewey's lieutenant retorts.

Cold and hungry, a glum Holsie Colldren attempts a few small bites, then runs behind a boulder just in time for her bowels to expel everything stored in her intestinal tract.

"Like prunes through a goose," Dewey announces, then gobbles up what's left on Holsie's plate. "You either got the stomach for it or you don't."

Like a minimum-wage factory worker, someone is assigned the unenviable task of tending to the leaky flesh of my wound. From the sounds of things, my forehead now resembles a cauliflower patch of cracklin. I have no way of knowing what the others see.

I overhear Dewey telling someone that when I looked in his direction, he became hypnotized.

"Dude. He can hypnotize you just by looking at you!"

"Dewey, he's…blind." Amy?

The reality is that the third eye did not turn out to be any seal of redemption on my forehead. Just a lopsided bull's-eye on my face that I will wear forever.

And don't think the irony of this has been lost on me. The addition of a third eye hasn't increased my vision or given me special insights. It has left me with the inability to see anything at all.

Not only is my cable out, but my satellite dish is down as well. I have no reception whatsoever. My TV is kaput. For reals. Not even a test pattern.

It must be night. It's colder.

Nobody sleeps. Or maybe we all do.

Morning is night, but later…or earlier.

An advancing fire line forces us to move onward and upward, and my suspicion is that nobody bothers to extinguish our own campfire. We stumble, slip and slide, making our way west, following the sparkling bright eye of Venus.

I hear sirens from the future.

People complain in whispers that I am holding them back.

I see a smiling Duft, who was never listening at all—just waiting to speak. Even so, her words are still sugar-water candy-sweet.

When those honey-words of encouragement dissipate, Amy will change her name—again—and move to Gotham.

And Dewey? He's got a future ripping tickets at the Dunk Tank in Hardhit, Ohio.

Fa shizzle, fa rizzle.

The average American has 9.5 friends. Some of us get screwed, but that's how averages work. I try to do the math for everyone, but it's too difficult. Instead I provide them with the week's winning lottery numbers and the trifecta of next year's Preakness.

Never wanted this to turn into an undisciplined conclusion, or such a close-management situation, but, hey, we can either learn to live together in peace or all turn into great big fucking tuna fish and get caught in the nets with all the other dolphins. You gettin' it yet?

Never made it to Happy Valley either, but for twenty bucks I can read your aura and call out the names of your enemies and tell you if there is a sickness growing inside of you.

Cancer's the specialty, but here's another trick:

When somebody is telling the truth, they look to the left. When they lie, they always look to the right. Arching your eyebrows before speaking indicates a lie is about to be told. Pupil size remains constant when speaking non-truths, but the comfort of reality will betray you and your pupils will narrow into slits when it's for reals.

What a child sees, a child becomes.

What you think will be drawn to you.

Seven is the number of perfection.

You will never experience peace until you get rid of blame.

Somebody—I don't know who she is—keeps blabbing about her *déjà vu* as if she's been here before, but she hasn't. Any rodeo clown could tell her that she's experiencing cryptomnesia and dredging up forgotten memories from her own troubled past.

She prattles on incessantly about a class she took—interpersonal relationships—and now never uses the pronoun "you" because it's an attack word. Instead, she uses the collective "we," ingratiating herself into everybody else's business.

Her breath is salty and stale, inches from my good ear.

"We screwed up big time."

I don't like her.

Tactile, sport-fucking lookie-loos.

Where has all this running got me?

Scars and candy bars.

Unwhole, then whole again. Living on vapors.

Getting wiggy widdit.

Bomb-bad, baby.

Most of us missed our ride home, heads stuck someplace where there is very little light shining.

What's the rush? The world we live in has already fallen.

The great divine truths spellbind, then betray us.

Existence is suffering; the cause of suffering is desire. Some of us choose to suffer.

Careful what you wish for.

Somebody once told me I had a dangerous fate, and that's always intrigued me—until now. Today begins the search for the first day of the rest of my forever.

Everything old gets old again.

And then, the largest affront of all—nasal appraisal.

The collective stench opens up yet one more portal. Don't need eyes to know that they're standing before me in awkward silence, embarrassed. Smelling. Scratching. Their personal odor prints as distinctive as their voices.

A rustle of paper, followed by the blowback from Dewey's impious halitosis.

"Dude."

"Just read it to him," somebody says.

"I will." Dewey reads, "Here I sit, broken-hearted."

A thump. Probably a boot to Dewey's ass.

"It doesn't say that."

"I know," Dewey whines, "just trying to keep it real."

"Just read the fucking thing."

The reeking human known as Dewey leans even closer. As much as I want to hear what he has to say, I have to pull away.

The rattle of paper again.

But Dewey can't do it. He resigns the task. "Here. Somebody else."

Grunts, groans, more shuffling. Conspiratorial whispers. Whatever is written on the paper for me to hear will have to wait. Nobody wants the job of breaking the bad news.

Who then will read the words to save me? Not Duft.

"We have to go." Briola?

Something is pushed into my hands. A cup or a bowl.

"Dude. Here's some stew."

A voice in the distance says, "We're going."

Bob Bluitt orders his recruits to fall in. One can only assume the submissive Barbies do what they are ordered to do.

A crumpled wad of paper is pushed under my fingers.

Feet crunch over rocks and debris. I hear them leave, loud and crisp at first, then receding until it becomes utterly quiet.

Several hours later I speak for the first time.

"Where are the angels out there who will write my name in the Lord's Book of Life?"

There is no response. Not even a whisper from the canonized Brahulyo Saucedo. Where did he go?

Somewhere off in the distance, a thumping *whump-whump* coming from Pepper Ranch. Maybe they're bombing the place. Who knows. Maybe the Big Ship did come, like Beth promised it would, and maybe the U.S. government couldn't handle it and, fearful that the promise of salvation would lead to panic and anarchy, they did what they do best—they destroyed it, along with the curious and those who came to believe in it.

Outside, everywhere, in the dark, chanting.

Beth, you still there? I forgive you.

The last of the puppy stew was passed weeks ago. Painted with poop, I rapidly dissolve into a composted pile of worthless human crap-mulch. Roses won't grow here. But salmonella, shigellosis and hepatitis-A, take on a life of their own.

Someone kind leaves a radio, but the batteries too desert me and I'm left wondering if the Rockies managed to weather the rain delay and came back to beat the Giants.

On my new planet of etherized disarrangement, the world reappears slow as seeping water. An apprehensive wind, restless in the dark, thrashes in place. A comet streaks past—orange flashes, sparklers.

I count out loud to a million, then start over again.

A long Asian moon flutters, unopened, floating deeper and deeper, turning interior, floating deeper still.

And how many times will I have to hear that if you don't like the weather, wait five minutes and it will change?

Well, it's become warm again. Very little breeze.

When it's cooler, usually in the morning, shimmering heat waves billow from my forehead/face-thing, but anything even remotely viewable has been forever obscured by my eye-deadened pixilation. So what's the point?

I dream of cotton sheets, clean and pressed; a pillow. Wonder what words of wisdom are scrawled on the piece of paper in my pocket.

When the wind is right, I smell something musky sweet and sensual. Duft's horripilation immediately comes to mind. Is she watching from somewhere? Maybe sitting on a rock, holding her breath, daring not to make a sound, still seducing me with her pheromones.

It could be Amy. It could be Candy, for all I know.

Perhaps it's Kwame, last seen sporting a high-top fade, standing stoic, like some great Nubian protector, feet and shoulders squared—militant, menacing, magnificent.

Maybe nobody's there. I can usually tell. The newbies come alone or with tour groups, and they all want to know the same thing.

Rise, fall. Step aside.

But I can't do any of those things.

Satanic demons entered my spirit and I embraced them. From the son of the devil to the child of the Lord, I was open to correction and given a warning—live in peace. Repent to Him and bury the bone. Bask in the glory of His presence or the anointing will never be released. Trust me on this.

The agonies of my own satellite of flower dreams, once curled up in the silky beauty of twilight song, are now dished up and served indiscriminately to hungry cast members, living proof that even a blind pig manages to stumble across a fallen acorn once in a while.

Me so hungry.

Somebody takes my shoes and pants.

Dark things move through the brush, unidentifiable.

Things bite me, chew on me when I fall asleep.

But still they come—the curious and mindless alike, snapping pictures, asking questions. Staring. Paying unholy homage, leaving behind a few coins, occasionally a bill or two. Usually they just want to know what's written on the paper. They steal more than they offer.

Take, just take. But go away.

To ask for help is a sin, and it's a relief when they get what they want and leave. Somebody donates a few power bars, a bottle of water. A smelly stranger will come by later and take it all.

Think. Breathe. *Listen.*

Just like Brahulyo Saucedo, the potential is there in each and every one of us to be a saint. If people would just care for one another.

Benighted, I see witches here. Devils, macabre things. Not every day, but more often than not. Star-whispers, a shrieking moon, energy states floating above ground. I know the colors of all those sounds.

Imagine: I could have been coffee-cigarettes-a-car, stammering beer-bright into the pulse of dead space, able to use no door, weaving and shaking hysterically in cold, flat immurement.

But no.

Here, in this secret interior, everything is all so different. Here, all night, the stars whisper thick with blood my name over and over again until, burnt-eyed-burst, mantra-chant-hammered forth, I erupt, stammer full-face in their awe and give them, so they might go, reasons for reasons; blood, matter, air.

What could be slower than this: the dirt breathing hard beneath my feet, hours drunk on the stultifying silence, the changing of the seasons. The practiced ease of listening to one lung scuffle, the rattle of dried leaves pressing into shapes mystical beyond belief, shrunken into beaten sleep. Waiting out the dream thing.

All this running. And what has it got me.

Unwhole, then whole again.

The thundering joy of oneness.

Zero to sick, see?

One. Two. Three.

The only message that matters: We come from where we started, we go to where we are.

End of story.